Dear MyTime Young Carer,

I wrote this book because I think Young Carers are awesome, and deserve out-of-this-world alien adventures!

I hope you have a very merry Christmas, and enjoy this story.

If you do enjoy it, perhaps you could make up your own story – including aliens, or unicorns, or dragons, or robots, or whatever else you think is cool. Maybe it could all take place in Dorset, or on the Isle of Wight?

You could write it like I do, or draw a comic, or make storyboards and scripts for a film or TV show. The important thing is getting it out of your head, and onto the page.

Or you can also just enjoy reading stories, and exercising your imagination!

Merry Christmas,
Rab

THE LATE CREW

AND THE

COPY CAT CREATURE

RAB FERGUSON

VP

Valley Press

First published in 2024 by Valley Press
Woodend, The Crescent, Scarborough, UK, YO11 2PW
valleypressuk.com

ISBN 978-1-915606-41-9
Cat. no. VP0235

Illustrations by Valeriia Proskurina.
Cover and text design by Jamie McGarry.

THE MIRROR MOUSE

It was a quiet night in Morfield Woods. The only sound was the wind rustling through leaves and grass. The stars twinkled overhead, and it was dark between the trees. Somewhere, one owl called out '*tooo-whiit*', and another replied '*tooo-wooo*'.

Then there was a bright flash of light above. It was followed by a rather unusual whistling sound, like a firework falling out of the sky.

Whissss
          ssss
                ssss
                      ss
                         ss
                         ss
                         BAMF

A meteor the size of a beach ball slammed into the dirt, glowing orange with heat. Leaves twirled down from the nearby trees, shaken off their branches by the impact.

Hours passed, and the rock cooled down, the orange colour darkening to black. It looked like a large piece of coal, with several holes in it. For a long time, the animals in the woods stayed back from this strange object that had fallen from the sky.

Eventually, a mouse crept out from under the roots of a tree, sniffing curiously. The metallic scent in the air was like nothing the mouse had ever smelt before.

A scratching sound came from inside the meteorite. The mouse froze, its little heart beating very fast. Something was moving in there.

Scritch-scritch-scritch-scritch

From one of the holes, a new mouse emerged, curls of strange silvery smoke rolling out with it. The new mouse looked *exactly* like the old one, from the bend in its whiskers to the brown shade of its fur.

It was a perfect copy.

Seeing this mirror image of itself was too much for the original mouse. It let out a petrified squeak, then fled, disappearing into the forest. The copy-mouse crawled through Morfield Woods, heading towards the town.

HIDING UNDER HUGO

Alisha Alva was dreading today. She didn't even want to get out of bed. Especially since she'd have to move her cat, Hugo, who was curled up on her belly.

'You stay right there,' she whispered to Hugo. 'I'll hide under you all day.'

The black-and-white cat purred, stretching out his front legs. He looked like he'd be *purr*-fectly happy with that plan.

'Except I can't,' said Alisha, frustration rising in her voice. 'Because my stupid Head of Year, Miss Penn, wants to have a *chat* with me today, about if I'm *doing* OK. You know what that means, don't you?'

Hugo watched her lazily. Sometimes it almost felt like he could understand what she was saying. He was a better listener than any human she'd met, even Mum.

'It means I have to speak to her, and act like a ♫ *very normal perfectly proper girl* ♫,' Alisha sing-songed. 'Because if I don't act like a ♫ *very normal perfectly proper girl* ♫ then Miss Penn will say I'm not *doing OK*. She might even say I'm *having a difficult time*. That'd mean teachers being weird with me. They never want to just treat you normally, teachers.'

Alisha scratched behind Hugo's ear, and he nuzzled his head into her hand. That was the best thing about her furry companion – she could tell him anything, ever, and he'd never treat her any different. Not as long as she kept feeding and fussing him.

She'd even told Hugo about last term, when she and her friends, The Late Crew, found an alien egg. They'd looked after it till it hatched into a baby dragon and flew away in a spaceship with its dad.

She also told him about the slime that

had taken control of her headteacher, and how they'd beaten it with loud music. Alisha hadn't told anyone else about the aliens, not even Mum.

'Maybe I should tell Miss Penn about the aliens,' Alisha joked to her cat. 'She'd definitely put me down as *having a difficult time* then!'

Was there another, even worse, category for if you said you saw aliens? Maybe *not doing very well at all* or *really struggling quite a bit indeed.*

'You know what the worst part is?' said Alisha, sitting up under Hugo. The cat turned his body to make himself even more comfortable. 'The worst part is the reason Miss Penn wants to talk is that teachers have noticed I've been quiet in lessons. Quiet! Me! They've spent all year telling me to talk less. As soon as I do, they say there's something wrong!'

Hugo started to close his eyes again. Alisha couldn't let him go back to sleep – she did actually need to get up and go to school now, no matter how much she didn't want to. There was only one thing she could say that would get him up and going.

'Breakfast time!'

MUM IN PEACE

Alisha buttered her toast, while Hugo munched happily in the corner. Of course she fed the cat before herself!

She didn't want to think about her *chat* with Miss Penn. Instead, she was trying to focus on looking forward to seeing The Late Crew after school. They met up at least once a week and talked about whether they'd spotted any signs of aliens returning to Morfield. So far, there'd been nothing. Utterly zilch.

'*Boo!*' shouted Mum, jumping into the kitchen in her pink pyjamas. Their flat was half the size of her friends' houses but with the way Mum leapt and danced around, it never felt small. Mum had dark hair and dark eyes like Alisha, and a face full of mischief. She was a young mother, and people sometimes thought she was Alisha's older sister.

'You scared me,' drawled Alisha sarcastically. 'I thought you were a creature from outer space.'

'**I COOOOOME IN PEEEACE**,' Mum said, doing her best alien impression. She never cared about being proper or sensible. If something might be funny, she'd do it to make you laugh.

'There's nothing peaceful about you,' Alisha quipped.

'I don't want to be peaceful anyway. It's boring!' pouted Mum. 'You've got aliens on the mind recently. Want me to make you a tin-foil hat? You'd fit right in at my support group.'

'*Muuuuuuum*,' groaned Alisha.

'*Whaaaaaat?*' said Mum, imitating the way Alisha said it.

'You're not supposed to say things like that. Your support lady said.'

'Oh, well then,' Mum said, then put on her well-behaved voice. '*I will not say bad things about mental health problems, in case I start to believe them about myself. I will not make brilliant jokes, no matter how naturally hilarious I am.* Is that better?'

'Shush,' replied Alisha, but she grinned as she said it. Mum had difficulties with her thoughts and feelings, which were called mental health problems – though Mum called them her Letters. Not everyone liked jokes about mental health, but Mum found it really funny to joke about serious things.

'We'd better get you to school,' said Mum. 'You've got your super exciting chat with your favourite ever Head of Year today.'

'Ugh, don't remind me.'

Alisha hadn't actually told Mum the full truth about why Miss Penn wanted to talk to her. Mum thought it was another conversation about being too loud in class – not one about being too quiet. Little did Alisha know, this was only the start of her problems. Something much weirder than she could imagine was already on its way.

THE TRIPLE P: PINK PYJAMA PROBLEMS

'Wait a second,' said Alisha, as Mum picked up her car keys and headed towards the door.

'Aren't you ready to go?' asked Mum.

'I am, but you're not!' exclaimed Alisha.

'What do you mean?' Mum was utterly perplexed.

'You're still in your pyjamas!'

Mum laughed, looking down at her pyjamas which consisted of a fluffy pink top and bottoms – obviously not outdoor clothes.

'Oh, well.' Mum shrugged. 'I'm not working at the shop till twelve. I'll pop my jacket on over the top, no one will see.'

'There'll be teachers there, when you drop me off,' protested Alisha. If Miss

Penn found out Mum dropped her off in her pyjamas, she'd think Alisha had *problems at home* and was *not OK*.

'I'm sure no one will notice,' replied Mum, pulling her jacket on. 'We don't want you getting in trouble for being late again.'

Alisha didn't know how to explain the problem. Mum was thinking about it like she was any other parent. But the school knew about Mum's Letters. Sometimes when people knew about Mum's mental health it made them see her differently, in a way that was completely unfair.

For example: if they saw another parent doing drop off in their PJs, they'd think *how funny, they must have been in a rush.* But if they saw Alisha's mum doing it, they'd think *that's the mum with mental health issues, she can't even get dressed in the morning.*

The most unfair thing was, Mum was doing really well with her Letters. She was working with a woman from a charity, learning ways to manage when she had bad days and felt really sad or angry. But no one ever thought about that.

How could Alisha possibly tell her that the school saw her differently to other parents? It would hurt her feelings, and it wasn't Mum's fault that other people got the wrong idea.

'You're right, let's go,' said Alisha, giving in.

She'd just have to hope no one saw Mum's pink pyjamas, and make sure that Miss Penn thought everything was as ♫ *very normal perfectly proper* ♫ as possible!

KEEP DRIVING, GO ON THE RUN, BECOME OUTLAWS

'Shall we just drive past the school?' teased Mum, while they sat in slowly moving traffic. 'Go to the shopping centre instead?'

Mum was joking but Alisha knew that if she agreed, they'd most likely end up actually doing it. She and Mum had skived and gone shopping together before. Mum had called her job and pretended to be sick, then done the same with Alisha's school.

That day had been so fun, simply because they were breaking the rules. The shopping centre was out of town, and everyone they knew would either be at work or school – but Alisha and Mum still giggled and snuck from shop to shop as if someone was about to catch them.

'I'm very tempted to say yes,' admitted Alisha.

'Probably better not, with your chat with Miss Penn today,' Mum replied reluctantly, tapping her fingers on the steering wheel. Her fingernails were still red from when Alisha had painted them at the weekend.

'You're right,' sighed Alisha, even though shopping sounded infinitely better than talking to the Head of Year. 'But we have to do it again sometime!'

'I'm a bad influence on you,' Mum laughed.

They stopped at a red light and Mum looked over with a rare serious expression on her face. Alisha felt like everything became a bit quieter when Mum got serious, as if the world missed her silliness.

'Are you alright for school today? It was a late one last night,' said Mum.

The night before was one of Mum's Bad

Nights. Tiredness from Bad Nights was the real reason Alisha had been quiet in school recently. She could try explaining why she needed to stay up late and make sure Mum was OK, but she didn't think the Head of Year would understand. She'd have better luck explaining her alien adventures!

'I'll be alright,' said Alisha. 'You're going to buy me a cappuccino at the ChocoHut drive-through before school, right?'

Mum snorted, driving forward as the traffic lights turned green. 'No chance you'd order anything other than a hot chocolate at ChocoHut. And you know my opinion on coffee.'

'Which is?' asked Alisha, pretending to be innocent.

'It only wakes you up because it makes you need to poo!'

Mum laughed at herself, and it was like the lights being switched on at Christmas. Suddenly she was happy and sparkly again, all seriousness disappearing away behind bright colour. Alisha liked it best when Mum was like this. Because who wouldn't be happy when looking at Christmas lights?

At the corner where Mum needed to turn right for Morfield Secondary School, she turned left instead and parked by the newsagent. She was still smiling about the coffee and didn't look like she'd noticed she'd parked in the wrong place.

'Erm, Mum?'

'You can get out here,' she said to Alisha, speaking gently. 'Cross the road and then you're at school. You won't need to worry about me embarrassing you in my pyjamas.'

Alisha hesitated, her face going red. She didn't want Mum to think she was embarrassed by her. But she also didn't want someone to see Mum's pyjamas and tell Miss Penn.

'It's OK,' said Mum. 'Your grandmother used to embarrass me on purpose when I was your age. I hated it.'

'I'll walk from here,' said Alisha, picking up her school bag and climbing out. 'But I'm really *not* embarrassed by you.'

Mum nodded, and Alisha closed the car door. When she drove away, Alisha felt an uncomfortable knot in her stomach. She hoped Mum knew she'd never be ashamed of her, no matter what she was wearing or doing. It was other people and their reactions that were the problem!

Alisha was lost in thought as she walked towards the school steps, trying to think of something nice she could do for Mum that night. She didn't pay any attention to the pigeon pecking at crumbs on the road. Or to the exact copy of that pigeon, which flapped down and landed next to it. The copy had identical markings, almost as if there was a mirror between the two birds.

The copy-pigeon bobbed along after Alisha ... following her towards the school.

A BOTHERSOME RECEPTIONIST AND A CLEVER PIGEON

Alisha joined the crowd filing into the school. She walked beside a group of older teenagers, carefully keeping them between herself and the reception desk.

Recently, the receptionists had been trying to speak to her every morning when she came in. There were other kids they picked out each day as well. She thought teachers probably asked them to keep an eye on students they were worried about. Alisha didn't want to be worried about. She just wanted to be left alone.

'Alisha Alva! How are you today?' called out a nasally male voice from reception.

Alisha ground her teeth, irritated. It was Mr Cuthbert, one of the receptionists. He had a pointy face and wore square glasses. How did he always spot her? She was tempted to not go over, but he'd keep on speaking to her anyway. If she had to talk to him, it was better up close than shouting over people's heads.

She walked up to the reception desk. There were signs about the school's values propped up on it, about things like being *respectful* and *organised*. Nothing on there about being a *good laugh*, much to Alisha's disappointment. Mr Cuthbert was tall, so even though he was sitting she was still looking up at him a little.

'Did you walk in today?' Mr Cuthbert asked, trying too hard to sound casual. 'I didn't see your mum dropping you off?

Every day this week, the receptionists had asked questions about Mum. Alisha knew they weren't just asking. They were looking for any changes that might mean she was *having a difficult time* at home.

'She dropped me off across the road,' said Alisha, and then lied rather than mentioning Mum's pyjamas. 'The school car park was busy.'

Alisha was finding it easier and easier to lie to the school staff. She was even able to meet Mr Cuthbert's eye as she said it. Lying was the only way to get them to back off. Especially when the minute she said something even ever-so-slightly out of the ordinary they started inspecting her like an animal at the zoo.

'Cool, cool,' replied Mr Cuthbert, resting one elbow on the reception desk as if saying cool made *him* really cool. 'And how's it hanging?'

'No one says "how's it hanging" any more,' quipped Alisha. 'Not since phones looked like bricks and people watched movies on videotape.'

Making snarky comments had got Alisha in trouble in the past, but she knew the teachers had said she was being quieter than usual. So, if she wanted the school to think everything was normal and stop bothering her, then the best thing to do was act like her typical sarcastic self.

'Well, I'm glad you've got your sense of humour back,' commented Mr Cuthbert. But then he added a second elbow onto the desk and leant on his chin. 'But really, how *have* things been going?'

He looked at her like he couldn't wait to hear more about her life. Luckily, she was saved from having to answer by an unexpected arrival.

'Alisha!' It was Tyler, one of her friends from The Late Crew, breathing hard as he rushed into reception. His hair was messy, and his shirt was untucked. He'd probably run here after dropping his little brother Levi off at primary school.

'Hi, Tyler,' she said, turning gratefully away from Mr Cuthbert and following her friend towards the main school building. The receptionist called something after her about talking again tomorrow, but she thought she could get away with ignoring it.

'You still coming round later?' Tyler asked, as they went to their lockers. 'Levi's very excited for another *Late Crew: Alien Activity Watch* hang out.'

It had been Alisha's idea to call their hang outs *Alien Activity Watch*, which they said dramatically like it was the title of a TV show. Unfortunately, since they'd first met aliens, there'd been no further signs of alien activity whatsoever.

'I'm coming,' Alisha replied, opening her locker and putting books in her bag. 'If I don't run away and join the circus to avoid my chat with Miss Penn today.'

'Oh, *The One Who Doesn't Understand*,' said Tyler, using his nickname for Miss Penn. 'That'll be so much fun for you.'

'An absolute barrel of laughs, I'm sure,' she scoffed. 'It'll be me and the Head of Year, trading banter and jokes. And it's halfway through science, one of the lessons I actually enjoy! Couldn't it at least have been maths?'

'I like maths,' said Tyler.

'Well, someone has to, I guess.'

Unknown to them, as they talked, the two friends were being watched. On the outside ledge of the window behind them, the copy-pigeon sat and stared inside, a quite un-pigeon-like intelligence in its eyes.

IF ONLY ALISHA WAS A COLOUR-CHANGING FISH

'It can be very useful for animals to be hard to see,' said Mr McNulty. 'It helps prey avoid being eaten. And it helps predators sneak up on prey to eat!'

Alisha was annoyed that science was the lesson she had to leave early. They were studying biology that term, and it was interesting learning about different animals. She liked how excited Mr McNulty got about it all. Plus, he wrote a list of animal facts on the white board each week – some of which were pretty cool!

'When an animal is camouflaged, it blends in with its environment.' Mr McNulty held up a textbook, open on a photo of a white wolf. 'Arctic wolves are hard to see, because they're the same colour as the snow.'

'The wolf's camouflage can't be that good, sir,' piped up Alisha.

'Why's that?'

'Because we can all see it!'

The rest of the class laughed.

'Well, humans have fancy cameras,' explained Mr McNulty, taking no notice of the sniggering. 'But if you're an arctic bird, flying along and not paying attention, then...'

SNAP! Mr McNulty closed the textbook to illustrate a wolf's jaw snapping. That was another reason Alisha liked him. He didn't tell you off for making a joke, he just went along with it.

'Actually Alisha, don't you need to be going?' asked the science teacher.

Alisha nodded and started gathering her things. She could feel everyone looking at her. They'd want to know why she was allowed to leave early.

'Where are you going?' demanded a girl called Patsy, twisting around in her chair to stare at Alisha. Patsy was the biggest gossip in their year. Her and Alisha weren't friends, but Patsy was nosy about everything.

'I've got to see Miss Penn. Apparently I make too many jokes in class.'

After Alisha's wolf joke, Patsy would believe that. She'd tell the rest of the class, which would stop any other rumours about why she needed to talk to Miss Penn. Making jokes was sort of like camouflage for Alisha. As long as she was being funny, no one would realise that the teachers thought she wasn't *doing* OK.

When Alisha left, she made sure to give a few people a cheeky grin. That way they'd definitely think she was just in trouble for messing around too much. Once the door closed behind her, she listened to Mr McNulty getting on with the lesson.

'The arctic wolf's camouflage only

works in its own habitat. If you put one in a jungle, it'd stick out like a big white sore thumb. A few special animals can disguise themselves anywhere, like cuttlefish that change colour...'

Alisha wanted to stay and hear more about cuttlefish. But she also wanted to convince Miss Penn to leave her alone, and being on time would be a good start!

Mr McNulty's Animal Facts

Week: Nine

Topic: Hiding in plain sight

A mimic octopus changes its shape and the way it swims to pretend to be other sea animals. It can even swim like a jellyfish or flatfish.

Chameleons are lizards that change colour. People used to think it was for camouflage, but actually they mostly change colour to show their emotions – like a mood ring!

Owl butterflies have a pattern like an owl's eyes on their wings, which scares off small birds that might try to eat them.

A puff adder is a snake that doesn't only camouflage how it looks, it also camouflages how it smells – so dogs and meerkats can't sniff it out!

Leaf insects look almost exactly like a leaf, which makes them extremely hard to spot when they're standing on a tree branch.

Even lions are camouflaged. Have you ever thought about how they are the same sandy colour as their surroundings? It helps them to hunt.

EVERYTHING'S MORE INSPIRING WHEN THERE'S A PICTURE OF A MOUNTAIN

Alisha knocked on Miss Penn's door.
She had a new office this term, after her
old one nearly collapsed with Alisha and
the rest of The Late Crew inside. That
had been the beginning of their alien
adventures.

'Come in,' said the prim voice inside.
Alisha opened the door and saw the Head
of Year sitting at her desk. There was a
poster of a mountain behind her, with
'Climb as high as you can dream' written
in the sky. It was meant to be motivational,

but Alisha thought it didn't really make sense.

'Hi, Alisha. Why don't you take a seat?'

Alisha sat down opposite her. The Head of Year was stiff and serious. Her neat blonde hair was tucked into a bun, and she wore a black blazer over her white shirt. Alisha couldn't imagine Miss Penn dancing around, pulling faces and being silly, like Mum.

'How are you doing today, Alisha?'

I'd pay a million pounds to stop everyone asking me that, thought Alisha. *Actually, if I had a million pounds, I'd buy an island for me and Mum to live on. Then I wouldn't need to worry about school and people asking annoying questions.*

'I'm good, thanks,' said Alisha instead. Telling Miss Penn what she'd do with a million pounds probably wouldn't seem very ♫ *perfectly proper* ♫.

'Would you like a cup of tea?' Miss Penn offered.

'Er, no thanks.'

Alisha was taken aback. She'd been in Miss Penn's office loads of times before and had never been offered a drink. To be fair, she was usually there because she'd been told off. The Head of Year probably didn't want to reward bad behaviour with cups of tea.

'So, why do you think I wanted to talk to you today?' Miss Penn's voice was sweeter than usual. It was like she was trying to pretend she wasn't the same person that told Alisha off most days for wearing jewellery in school.

'Because teachers have said they've missed my quick-witted sense of humour in lessons?' suggested Alisha.

Miss Penn actually laughed. 'Well, sort of. We've noticed you've not been quite yourself recently.'

'I used to get in trouble for making too many jokes,' pointed out Alisha.

'We do look out for changes in your mood, but that's only one part of it. A few teachers have mentioned you've been very tired. Mrs Birk said you were falling asleep in English.'

Alisha gulped. She sat at the back of the class in English. The other day she had struggled to keep her eyes open after a Bad Night with Mum. She thought no one had noticed.

'It's not my fault Mrs Birk's teaching puts me to sleep,' said Alisha, trying to be funny again. But her voice wobbled, and she knew she didn't sound as confident as before.

This time Miss Penn didn't smile. 'Have you been getting enough sleep, Alisha?'

She didn't want to tell Miss Penn why she'd been staying up late. Then they'd definitely describe her as *having a difficult time*. They'd probably even say she had *problems at home*.

'I get plenty of sleep,' Alisha lied. 'So does my cat. He'd sleep all day, if he could.'

'Hmm,' said Miss Penn, as if she didn't believe her. 'Can you think of any reason you've been so tired?'

Miss Penn had started the conversation as if she was trying to be nice. Now it felt like an interrogation!

'Well, I'm almost a teenager.' Alisha shrugged. 'Maybe hormones?'

Alisha had never one hundred percent understood what hormones were but teenagers seemed to blame them for everything, so it was worth a try!

'We want to make sure you're OK, and awake enough to learn,' pressed on Miss Penn.

Alisha thought *awake enough to learn* was probably the Head of Year's priority!

'I'll try my best to be my usual energised self,' said Alisha, attempting to sound sincere. She hoped that would be the end of it, and she could leave.

'We want to make sure you have all the help you need, at home and at school.' Miss Penn handed Alisha a folded piece of paper. 'This is an invitation for you and your mum to come in after school next week for a meeting about how best to support you.'

Alisha put the note into her bag. Miss Penn said they were invited, like being invited to a party, but this felt more like an order. Miss Penn would ask about Alisha being tired, and Mum would have to explain all about her Bad Nights. It'd make Mum feel guilty and awful about her Letters, and the school would never treat Alisha normally again.

This was even worse than when it was just a *chat*. Now, she had an official *after-school meeting* with Miss Penn, with Mum there too. She needed a plan to get out of it, and fast!

MUM'S LETTERS

Mum always called her mental illness her 'Letters'. She'd even once written Alisha a letter about her Letters!

It was Mum's support lady from the charity who'd suggested doing that. Alisha thought it was a great idea, because now she could read it whenever she wanted to. She kept the letter in a drawer by her bed and read it at times when she wanted to understand Mum better.

Dear Alisha,

I'm writing you this letter to help explain my Letters (that's a dead clever way of starting, isn't it?)

My Letters are EUPD. The doctor gave them to me. It stands for Emotionally Unstable Personality Disorder, but that's long and difficult to remember — that's why I call them my Letters!

EUPD is a mental illness. That means it makes a difference to <u>how I feel, how I think</u>, and <u>the things I do</u>. I like to draw it as a triangle:

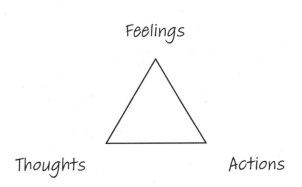

I'll draw it again, and explain how my Letters can affect each one.

Feelings

My feelings are very BIG! And they can change quickly.

I can go from feeling super happy — to super angry — to super sad, in just a few minutes.

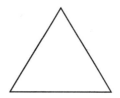

Thoughts

Sometimes my thoughts upset me, if I think about something bad that might happen.

Like that time I got scared you wouldn't talk to me anymore when you grow up! (but I know you will really, because I'm the coolest Mum ever)

Actions

Sometimes when my feelings get BIG, I find it hard to control what I do. It's why I've broken plates or cups before, and got a bit shouty.

Because of this, I have to look after myself and try to calm myself down if I'm not feeling good.

Because my Letters make me think, feel and act a bit differently, I can find it hard to understand other people — and they can find it hard to understand me!

That's why I wrote you this letter about my Letters (I liked it so much I said it again). But you can always talk to me as well, because I LOVE a natter.

From,
The One
The Only
Simply the best,
Mum xx.

ALIEN IN-ACTIVITY

'Hi everyone,' announced Tyler. 'Welcome to our *Late Crew: Alien Activity Meeting*. The date is Wednesday 21st February.'

Alisha was sitting on the floor in Tyler and Levi's shared bedroom, where once an alien egg had been hidden! The Late Crew sat together in a circle, drinking orange juice Tyler's Mum had brought them. As well as Alisha, there was:

- **Jayden,** who acted grumpy and tough. The other kids at school all believed it, but Alisha knew he was nice deep down.
- **Grace,** who was quiet and smart. She studied a lot, and somehow seemed to be good at *every* subject. Alisha didn't know how she was able to focus on everything at once.

- **Tyler,** who loved excitement and adventure. He and Jayden argued loads, but Alisha reckoned that was because they were both similarly stubborn.
- **Levi,** who was Tyler's little brother. He was younger than the rest and went to Morfield Primary School. He was clever too, in a different way than Grace. Alisha thought he must be the world's leading expert in all things to do with outer space!

Jayden, Grace and Tyler were young carers, like Alisha – that meant young people who helped look after family members. Levi was autistic and followed certain routines each day, which Tyler helped him with. They all became friends last year, after they first met aliens.

'I don't know why we have to say the date and everything,' complained Jayden. 'It's like school.'

'It was Levi's idea, to make it an official meeting,' replied Tyler, sounding annoyed.

'And it's a good idea. It helps make sure we don't miss any evidence of new aliens visiting.'

Levi smiled at his big brother.

Jayden rolled his eyes. 'None of us will have seen anything. It's the same every week.'

Tyler and Jayden would bicker for ages if Alisha didn't say something to stop it!

'Maybe we should schedule an hour each meeting for you two to argue?' said Alisha, in a sugar sweet voice. 'Then the rest of us could go and get ice cream while you do.'

Grace and Levi laughed, and Tyler and Jayden looked a little embarrassed. Alisha thought the two boys enjoyed arguing – and were actually good friends, beneath it all.

'You all know how the meeting works,' said Tyler, his face still a bit red. 'We go round the circle and say if we've seen anything unusual, or out of the ordinary, that might be a sign that aliens have returned to Morfield.'

'I've not,' said Jayden immediately.

'Me neither,' said Alisha with a shrug.

Grace held her pen over her notebook, waiting to write down anything they'd seen. It took her a moment to realise it was her turn. 'No, I haven't.'

'Neither have I,' added Levi, sounding utterly disappointed.

Tyler sighed. 'It's a no from me, too. Another week of nothing.'

They fell into a glum silence. Alisha couldn't help but look at Grace's notebook. Every page was blank, other than where Grace wrote the dates at the top. It had been so exciting when they first met aliens, starting with a four-legged creature called Runaway ... but that felt like a lifetime ago now.

'Runaway left the beacon in Morfield Woods,' said Levi. 'Letting aliens in trouble know they can come here for help. Someone will follow that signal eventually.'

Levi was right – there was a small

yellow flower in Morfield Woods that was supposed to be sending a signal out into space. Alisha looked at the others. She could tell they were all wondering the same thing: *why had no more aliens come?*

'Maybe the flower's broken?' suggested Grace.

'Or aliens have better places to go than crumby Morfield,' grumbled Jayden.

'We'll see aliens again though, won't we?' Levi asked his older brother. Levi had loved meeting extraterrestrials the most out of all of them.

'I ... I don't know,' responded Tyler. 'I really hope so.'

It was a horrible thought. What if The Late Crew never met another alien?

HUGO AND OGUH!

After *Alien Activity Watch*, Alisha headed home. The Late Crew had all cheered up a bit after playing a Jungle Magic board game. Grace had suggested not playing anything that included aliens, as that would be too much of a bummer.

It was nearly 5 p.m., and already getting dark. Alisha liked living in Morfield, where she was always within walking distance of her friends' houses. She couldn't imagine growing up in a big city!

Alisha and Mum's flat had a blue door, which opened on to stairs. They lived above an old man – so it was like one house split into a bottom and a top. When she arrived home today, she was surprised to see Hugo sitting in front of their blue door.

That was strange. Mum would be at work at the shop, and because they didn't have a cat flap, they normally only let Hugo out if they'd be around to let him back in. For a moment, Alisha thought it must be a different cat.

But no, as she got closer, she saw it was definitely Hugo. He had that white patch under his whiskers, and the other one on his neck. He meowed as she approached, like he'd been waiting for her to open the door.

'What are you doing out here?' questioned Alisha, scratching behind his ears. She unlocked the door, and Hugo climbed the stairs with her. There was no sign of Mum – she was definitely at work.

Then something even stranger happened. As they reached the top of the stairs, she heard a *meow* from the kitchen. *Wait, what!?* she thought. *There's already a cat inside?*

Out from the kitchen trotted… Hugo?? There were two Hugos!

The two identical cats froze as they spotted each other. Their fur stood on end, and their tails went big and puffy. They were exactly the same, as if Hugo was looking at himself in the mirror.

Then Alisha realised. It was as if Hugo was looking at himself in the mirror. The cat who'd come in with her was the mirror image of her own cat. The white patch under his whiskers, and the one on his neck, were on the **left** rather than the **right**. Just like a reflection!

Hugo *hissssssed*, then leapt forward at the copy-cat. The copy-cat ran, fleeing down towards the door, closely followed by the real Hugo. They clattered, screeched and yowled down the stairs.

Alisha chased after them. At the bottom, she found the front door was somehow open once again! There was a weird metal smell in the air too. The original Hugo (his white patches on the right) stood, hair-raised and still *hissing* loudly. But the copy-cat was nowhere to be seen.

'Well,' Alisha said to the real Hugo, stunned. 'At least I've finally got something strange to tell The Late Crew about.'

A PURR-FECT DISGUISE

GUYS. I got home 🏠 and there was an exact copy of Hugo outside my door. I brought him in BUT Hugo was already inside! Double cat 🐱🐱
– ALISHAAA

Potential 👽 activity?? – ALISHAAA

Sounds like you saw another cat that looks like yours 🙆 not that weird
– JAY G

Sometimes you get two cats that look similar – GRACE_FUL

Noooooo you don't get it. The copy-cat didn't "look like" Hugo. He was the EXACT SAME. A mirror image. Same patches, same whiskers, same paws!! – ALISHAAA

Levi thinks it might be 👽 related. He said an alien could disguise itself to fit in on the planet it lands on
– TY/LER

At least the brothers seemed to understand that this was no ordinary cat! Levi's idea reminded Alisha of Mr McNulty's lesson, about how different animals use camouflage. Could the cat she'd brought inside her house really be a creature from another world?

Mr McNulty had said there were two reasons for camouflage. If it actually was an alien in disguise, it was either:

- a predator that wanted to sneak up on them
- prey trying to hide from *something else.*

Alisha didn't know which option was more frightening.

We should investigate. It's the first odd thing we've spotted. We could explore near yours, see if we find anything strange? ••
– GRACE_FUL

Levi agrees. He says if there's something 👽, it might leave clues behind that are unusual for 🌑. We could come tomorrow after school?
– TY/LER

I can't believe we're animal detectives now. But I'm in – JAY G

Animal Detectives sounds almost as cool as The Late Crew 😎 I can do tomorrow too, if that's OK for you Alisha? – GRACE_FUL

Sounds good. I'm going out now to
see if I can spot the copy 🐱 again
– ALISHAAA

Be careful! If it is an alien, you're by
yourself! – GRACE_FUL

Alisha would have liked the others to head
over straight away. Going out alone and
looking for what might be a space predator
in disguise was scary. But, as young carers,
the others in The Late Crew had family
members to look after, just like her with
Mum. It wasn't easy for them to visit
without planning it beforehand.

However, Alisha didn't want to wait till
tomorrow and possibly lose the chance to
find another alien. She looked up at Hugo,
who'd retreated to the top of the stairs. His
green eyes peeked nervously down, his tail
still swishing behind him. He'd really been
spooked by his mirror image – he didn't
look like he'd be moving from that spot
any time soon, let alone coming with her.

She'd just have to manage by herself. She turned on her phone's torch and headed towards the door. She was going to find that copy-cat!

WHAT'S BEHIND THE DOOR?

As Alisha reached for the door, the handle turned from the other side. She stopped, imagining the copy-cat returning. How had it managed to open the door when it left? Would it still look like a cat when the door swung open ... or something else?

The door opened. It was Mum, returning from work. Alisha examined her face as she put down her bag. Everything was the right way round. This was the real Mum, not a mirror image or copy! But how grumpy and angry she looked almost made her feel like a different person.

'Turn your torch light off,' Mum snapped. She seemed furious, like she was holding back from being even more angry. She didn't say hello, or bother to ask what

Alisha was doing.

Alisha knew immediately that Mum was having a Bad Night. It really was like Mum was replaced by someone else at times like this. She was normally a crackling fire: bright, and comforting, and warm. But some nights she became a biting, icy wind.

Mum stomped past her up the stairs, glaring ahead as if in a mood too terrible to even speak. When she acted like this, it made Alisha feel awful, as if it was her fault Mum was upset. Like if she just hadn't had her torch on, Mum wouldn't have been so annoyed. But she knew that wasn't true.

This was part of what it meant, Mum having Letters. Her big feelings must have started at work. She'd have been serving customers and pretending everything was fine, while inside feeling worse and worse. Mum said hiding her emotions like that made her feel like a balloon filling with air, about to pop.

Mum stormed into the kitchen and

Alisha heard her slamming things as she put them away. If she broke something while she was doing that, she'd either get really angry or burst into a flood of tears.

Alisha *really* wanted to go out and search for the copy-cat. If she didn't go now, she might never see it again. But if she went out, Mum would need to make herself feel better alone. Some nights, Mum was able to do that by listening to music or doing something else she enjoyed.

Other nights, she struggled, and the big feelings and bad thoughts got worse and worse. This could even lead to Mum calling an ambulance because she was scared she might do something that would hurt herself.

Alisha turned off her phone torch. The copy-cat would have to wait. She couldn't bear to leave, not when she knew she could help Mum feel better.

'Mum,' Alisha called, as she headed up the stairs. 'Do you want to watch *I Blooming Love You*?'

I Blooming Love You was one of their favourite rom-coms. It was about a woman who fell in love with a flower salesman, even though she was allergic to flowers. She kept sneezing and falling off things, like her bike into a lake full of fish!

'Alright,' grunted Mum, from the kitchen.

It was a blunt reply, but at least not a bad or angry reaction. Alisha knew that watching the film would start to make Mum feel better. It was amazing how much good a rather silly film could do!

Things that help when Mum is having a bad night

Put on one of our favourite films — preferably a romantic comedy where we can speak along with the funniest lines.

Play music — Mum is always happier with music on. Choose fun songs, or a radio station with pop music on.

Ask a ridiculous question — like 'if you could be any animal, what would you be?' or 'if you could have any superpower, which would you choose?'. We can talk about these for ages!

(Mum said if she could have any superpower, she'd choose being able to fly, so she could see the world how a bird does. That's pretty cool.)

Get Mum to play a card game — especially one of the silly ones we made up together, like throw-a-three snap. It's just the same as normal snap, but if you draw a three you have to throw it at the other person!

Just be there – Sometimes Mum doesn't want to do any of the things that make her feel better, and it's hard to know what to do. But her Letters bother her worst when she's by herself. Even just staying around helps.

Alisha yawned as she went into her bedroom. They'd watched both *I Blooming Love You* and *I Blooming Love You 2: Wedding Flowers*. Now it was late. She was going to be tired at school again tomorrow, but at least Mum was feeling a bit better.

Hugo was waiting for her. She was surprised to see that he was wide awake. Normally when she came to bed he was already snoozing – and she had to work out how to get the covers out from under him!

'Mum will be OK,' she said to the cat, trying to reassure herself. 'She smiled at that scene in the second movie where they all fell in the fountain. She'll be back to normal in the morning.'

She tried to scratch Hugo's ear, but he twitched nervously away. He stared past her and out into the hall. It was like he was keeping an eye out for danger.

'The copy-cat scared you, didn't it?' she said. 'That's fair. I don't know how I'd react if I met the mirror image of myself.'

Alisha reached towards her feline friend, extra slowly. He didn't move away as she brought her hand to his head and started gently stroking him. After a moment, he even started to purr.

'Don't worry,' she told Hugo. 'My friends and I are going to investigate the copy-cat tomorrow. The Late Crew are on the case!'

DOES ALIEN POO GLOW GREEN?

The next day, Alisha couldn't focus at school. She was tired from Mum's Bad Night, and all she could think about was searching for the copy-cat later. In fact, she was so distracted, she nearly walked straight into Miss Penn in the corridor!

'Hi, Alisha. Did you give your mum the invitation to our meeting?' she asked.

Alisha felt her face go red. There were lots of kids from her year around, getting things out of their lockers. She wished Miss Penn wouldn't bring up her meeting in front of everyone. Also, she'd completely forgotten about the note in her bag and Mum coming into school next week!

'Y-yeah, I did,' stammered Alisha. 'She's checking with work to see if she can make that date.'

Miss Penn gave her a Look, with a capital L. It felt like she knew Alisha wasn't telling the truth.

'If that time doesn't work, she can call me to rearrange for another day next week.'

Luckily, at that moment a group of Year 10s walked past with their shirts untucked. Miss Penn hurried after to tell them off for 'setting a bad example' for the younger children. Alisha breathed a sigh of relief once she was gone. The Head of Year was persistent. There was no way Alisha was getting out of having this meeting – or of telling Mum about it!

'This is Hugo,' announced Alisha to the rest of The Late Crew, who had come over to her house after school.

They were gathered around the cat, who was sitting on a kitchen chair. Mum was at her group and had an appointment with her support lady afterwards, so would be out for a while – meaning The Late Crew could speak openly about their secret alien adventures.

'He has a white patch on the *right* of his neck, and another white patch on the *right* under his whiskers,' said Alisha.

Hugo purred contentedly, happy to be the centre of attention. He seemed to have recovered from meeting his mirror image.

'Let me make sure I'm getting this *right*,' goaded Jayden. 'Hugo's white patches are on the *left* ... *right*?'

Alisha scrunched up a piece of paper and threw it at him. It bounced off Jayden's chest and landed below Hugo, who stared down at it as if to say *I'd hunt that if I wasn't so lazy*.

'What should we look for when we do our search?' asked Grace.

'Well, I was thinking...' Tyler began, but trailed off when he saw how everyone else was looking at him.

'Levi's the alien expert,' said Alisha firmly, and the others nodded.

Tyler shrugged his shoulders, looking grumpy, as if he'd thought he was about to say something really clever. But he stepped back to let his little brother speak.

'We need evidence that the copy-cat is not from this world,' said Levi. 'Watch out for paw prints that mysteriously change shape, or cat fur that stretches like elastic, or anything else weird like that! Especially try to find its poo – if it has alien poo rather than cat poo, that would give away its disguise.'

'As if we're actually going to look for poo.' Jayden shuddered.

'Anything you wanted to add?' Alisha asked Tyler, knowing full well he wouldn't have thought of any of that.

'Um … I was going to say, we should look for anything glowing green.'

Everyone waited for him to say more, but that was it.

'*Really* helpful,' drawled Jayden sarcastically. 'I'd never have thought to mention if I saw something literally glowing. I'd have thought that was totally normal.'

'Right then,' said Alisha. 'We know what we're looking for. Now, this might be the strangest sentence I'll ever say. Let's get out there and find some alien cat poo!'

DON'T MIND US, WE'RE JUST LOOKING FOR AN ALIEN THAT MEOWS

The Late Crew split up to conduct the search. There was the street itself to explore, as well as a grassy garden area behind Alisha's flat that a few houses backed on to. The group each went in a different direction, like this:

Tyler
(left side of
the grass)

The Grass

Levi
(right side of
the grass)

The Flat

Jayden
(down the
street to
the left)

The Street

Grace
(down the
street to
the right)

Alisha
(across the road)

Alisha felt pretty silly, inspecting the pavement for signs of an alien cat. So far, all she'd found were weeds growing up through cracks in the concrete. She kept expecting someone to come out of one of the houses and ask what she was up to. But when she glanced through the windows, people were too busy watching TV to worry about her.

If someone does ask what we're doing, Alisha thought, *I'll tell the truth and say we're looking for an alien cat. They'll think we're playing some imaginary game and leave us to it.*

Down the road to either side, she could see Grace and Jayden searching too. Well, Grace was, anyway. Jayden was mostly playing on his phone. He looked up and saw Alisha watching him, and she mimed breaking it in half.

Even from a distance, she saw his over dramatic sigh. Still, he put his phone away and started concentrating properly. Alisha focused back on her own patch of pavement, examining a dandelion that had grown on the edge of the gutter, hoping maybe an alien cat had rubbed along it. Like everything else, it appeared totally normal.

Dandelions made her think of Mum – they were her favourite flower. This was probably because people called them weeds, and Mum loved saying the opposite thing to everyone else.

Alisha hadn't figured out a way to escape her after-school meeting, which meant she was going to have to tell Mum about it. She *hated* the thought of explaining that school had noticed how exhausted she was. It'd make Mum feel bad about tiring Alisha out. But it wasn't like Mum chose to have her Letters, and her Bad Nights!

Anyone •• anything yet? – ALISHAAA

Now who's on their phone too much?
– JAY G

Shut up – ALISHAAA

Nothing yet. Though I did find 50p!
– GRACE_FUL

£ £ £ – JAY G

Levi found a hedgehog 🦔 but not
like a space hedgehog we don't think
– TY/LER

WAIT – TY/LER

I don't know if this is anything
– TY/LER

But there's two hedgehogs on the
grass 🦔🦔 Levi and I both think they
look the exact same – TY/LER

Stay right there. We're coming!!
– ALISHAAA

HOW DO YOU TELL IF A HEDGEHOG IS FROM SPACE?

'The problem is,' complained Jayden, 'hedgehogs all look the same anyway!'

The Late Crew were on the grass behind Alisha's flat, where two very similar looking hedgehogs ambled around under a tree. It was meant to be a shared garden between the different houses and flats, but Alisha rarely saw anyone out here. There was one lady who'd set up a washing line, and an elderly man who cut the grass sometimes, and that was it.

It was hard to tell for sure if the hedgehogs were identical. The Late Crew were standing back so they wouldn't scare the little creatures away, which made it more difficult. Alisha had spotted hedgehogs around here before, though it was unusual to see them in the daytime like this.

She thought perhaps she could detect that weird metal smell in the air, like there'd been after the copy-cat ran away. But she wasn't sure. Could one of these hedgehogs really be an alien? And if so, how were they going to work out which one?

'I'm not sure I agree. I think Hedgehogs can actually look quite different from each other,' said Grace. 'These two are the exact same size and colour.'

They all studied the two animals, trying to decide whether they were perfect copies or just similar. Then the silence was interrupted by –

YoOoOoOoOoOoOoOoOowoWow

Hugo was in the window of Alisha's flat, fur puffed up as big as possible, yowling down at the hedgehogs.

'Seems like he thinks one of them is the copy-cat,' said Alisha.

'I agree with Hugo,' said Levi, who was staring at the hedgehogs particularly intensely. 'You have to look at the details – and think of it like a mirror.'

The Late Crew's youngest member swung his finger back and forth between the two hedgehogs under the tree, pointing out little details:

'This one has a darker *right* paw – and this one has a darker *left* paw.

There's a bent quill on its *left* – and a bent quill on its *right*.

A long whisker to the *right* – and a long whisker to the *left*.'

It was hard for Alisha to believe either animal was anything but a normal hedgehog. But when she looked for the details Levi had pointed out, she saw what he meant. The hedgehogs were mirror images of each other, exactly how it had been with Hugo and the copy-cat!

'Looks like we've found the copy

creature,' said Tyler, who sounded convinced now. 'The big question is – how do we work out which is real, and which is the copy?'

'*If* one of these hedgehogs really is some kind of copying alien,' said Grace, emphasising the *if* like she wasn't sure at all. 'And we're not even sure how an alien could possibly do that – then the real BIG question is, why Alisha?'

'Huh!?' asked Alisha. She hadn't expected Grace to say that!

'Well, if we're right … first it copied Hugo, and tried to make you bring it into your flat. Then the copy-cat became a copy-hedgehog and stayed nearby. Especially as you've met aliens before, it doesn't feel like a coincidence…'

Alisha felt a shiver run up her back. What could a transforming alien want with her?

'There's no point standing around,' butted in Jayden, who got bored way too easily. 'It's like Levi said with the cat poo – we need to check if there's anything unusual about them.'

Jayden rushed suddenly towards the hedgehogs, arms out as if trying to pick one up. The spiky creatures fled, moving with surprising speed.

'You scared them!' hissed Grace.

Jayden ignored her, darting after the hedgehogs. They split different ways, one going left and the other right, then –

POOF! The hedgehog that went right vanished in a puff of silver smoke, which glittered in the air. A sparrow shot out from the cloud, flying towards Tyler and Levi. Tyler made a grab for the bird, and it flapped the other way before –

POOF! The sparrow disappeared in another silver cloud. A mouse thumped down on to the grass and scampered off in the opposite direction. The mouse was too fast for Levi, who attempted to scoop it up. Alisha and Grace both moved forward to prevent the rodent from escaping –

POOF! A copy-Hugo ran out from the

silver smoke, slipping between their legs. Alisha was used to the regular Hugo trying this trick and caught the copy-cat with her hand on its back. It yowled like the real Hugo would if he was hurt. She let go without thinking – it was hard not to, when the copy looked exactly like her own cat!

The copy-cat shot across the grass, and Alisha was sure they'd lost it. She was so annoyed at herself; it had tricked her with the meow! But the copy-cat stopped at the far end of the garden area, then let out a long **WHOOOOOOOOOOOOSSSH!** as a bigger cloud of silver smoke built around it.

Alisha saw a figure inside the silver smoke, about her own height. She felt a tingle of fear, the hair standing up on the back of her neck. The copy-cat had become a human!

ALWAYS CHECK THE GRASS FOR ALIEN LIFE FORMS

The silver smoke faded away, slowly revealing the girl standing on the other side of the grass. She was Alisha's size ... with Alisha's dark hair ... wearing Alisha's school clothes ... and she had Alisha's face. The copy-cat had become a copy of her!

Alisha took deep breaths, trying to push down the panic rising inside her chest, but it wouldn't go away. Her own mirror image was staring back at her. No wonder Hugo had been so upset.

'This is too weird,' whispered Tyler.

'It's fascinating,' breathed out Levi.

'How does it transform like that?' asked Grace.

'One Alisha was enough,' muttered Jayden. She shot him a scathing look.

The copy-Alisha stood there, unmoving. The real Alisha attempted to ignore the urge to get as far away as possible, as fast as possible. She couldn't run now, not when she had the chance to find out what on Earth (or off it) was going on!

'Who are you?' asked Alisha, trembling. 'Why did you try to get in my flat?'

'Too weird,' the copy-Alisha replied, in an exact replica of Tyler's voice. It was like a recording of Tyler had played from its mouth!

'Fascinating,' the copy-Alisha added, in Levi's voice now.

'How does it do that?' it asked, in Grace's voice.

'Who are you?' it said, in Alisha's voice.

She didn't really like hearing her own voice aloud. It sounded strange and different when it was outside of her own head! The Late Crew all kept their mouths tightly shut. No one wanted to speak, and have their voice imitated.

'One Alisha was enough...' said the copy-Alisha, in Jayden's voice. Then it repeated itself again, cutting out words each time. 'One Alisha was... One Alisha... Alisha... Alisha...'

Alisha felt so tense her stomach was beginning to ache. A bead of sweat slipped down the side of her face. What did this copy creature want with her?

'This is so freaky,' said Grace, then slapped her hands over her mouth as if she hadn't meant to speak.

The copy-Alisha opened its mouth, and they all waited for an imitation of Grace. Instead, when it next spoke, it sounded like all five of The Late Crew talking at once.

'The Difference Machine is coming.'

Then POOF! the white shape of a barn owl flew up from a silvery cloud. The owl glided away over the houses, disappearing like a ghost vanishing out of view. The Late Crew were left behind, stunned into silence. Faint wisps of metallic-smelling smoke still floated in the air around them.

Alisha looked in the windows of the flats and houses that backed on to this grass, like hers. There was no one watching, from any of them. There'd been a shapeshifting alien in their back garden and apart from The Late Crew, no one had even noticed it.

AN ALIEN BUNNY
WOULD BE NICE

'Why are all the aliens we meet so creepy?'
complained Jayden. 'There's no way I'm
getting to sleep tonight.'

The Late Crew were back in Alisha's
room. They were all a bit shaken, with pale
faces and nervous expressions. The only
exception was Levi, who was lost in deep
thought, presumably about the copying
alien they'd just met.

'It wasn't that creepy,' said Alisha,
acting like it was no big deal. 'It just
looked like me.'

'*Exactly*,' replied Jayden. 'What could
be worse?'

Alisha threw a pillow, which bounced
off Jayden's chest and landed on the floor.
Hugo stared down at it from the top of the

wardrobe. The cat had kept his distance since they'd come in, most likely able to smell the metallic smoke on their clothes. After meeting the copy-cat, he'd want to stay as far from that smell as he could!

'It would be nice to meet an alien that was cute and fluffy,' admitted Grace. 'Like an alien puppy. Without the ability to transform into something scary. Or say anything terrifying.'

'You're so brave,' Alisha said to Levi. 'I don't know how you never get frightened. If I'm honest, I was ready to run so fast I'd leave an Alisha-shaped cloud of dust behind.'

Tyler and Levi exchanged a look, and Alisha felt like she might have said something wrong.

'I do get frightened,' Levi corrected her. 'I was really frightened last term, when we met The Slime. Sometimes, people think because I'm autistic I don't have the same emotions as everyone else, but I do. I just show my feelings in a different way.'

Levi paused thoughtfully, then went on. 'Sometimes I *see* things differently too. The reason I didn't find the copy-cat scary was because it was running away from us.'

Levi had a point. Whatever that creature was, it had spent the whole time running from them! The way he described seeing things differently reminded Alisha of Mum – and how people misunderstood her too.

'I'm glad you think the way you do,' said Alisha. 'I was so focused on being afraid, I never even thought about how the alien might have been feeling! And sorry if it sounded like I was saying you're not able to feel scared. I didn't mean it like that.'

'That's OK,' said Levi, smiling. Alisha guessed he probably thought quite a bit about how his mind and feelings worked, just like Mum. If most people's brains seemed to operate in a different way to yours, then even understanding yourself could be difficult!

'We're missing something,' said Grace. Her alien notebook was open in front of her. She'd written loads in it now, though she'd left gaps across the page. 'We need a name for the creature. It's not only a copy-*cat* any more, is it?'

'But it is a copy-cat!' exclaimed Alisha. 'It copies everything. So the name still works.'

'Oh, I like that. Almost as good as calling ourselves The Late Crew,' said Grace. 'Hands up if you agree we should call this new alien the copy-cat?'

Everyone raised their hands in agreement. Grace wrote the word *copy-cat* into all the blank spaces that she'd left in the notebook.

'What's a Difference Machine?' asked Tyler.

The room fell deathly silent, and suddenly they all looked afraid once more. That was the question that none of them had wanted to ask. The alien had said '*The Difference Machine is coming*'. That didn't sound like a good thing.

'We learnt about camouflage in Mr

McNulty's science class,' said Alisha. 'Animals camouflage when they're hunting something, or hiding from something. The copy-cat ran away from us, so it doesn't seem like it was hunting us. So maybe it was hiding from the Difference Machine.'

'So, the Difference Machine might be something so horrible that an alien that can transform into anything is terrified of it,' said Jayden, then added sarcastically, 'How *wonderful.*'

That was not a comforting thought. An uneasy feeling ran through Alisha's body. Whatever the Difference Machine was, it was on its way. She almost imagined she could feel it approaching, like a shadow heading towards the Earth... and their little town of Morfield.

IS THERE HOT CHOCOLATE IN SPACE?

The door opened downstairs, and Alisha heard Mum coming in. She told The Late Crew that she'd be back in a minute and stepped out of her room. The others carried on talking as she shut the door behind her. She hoped they wouldn't say anything too loudly about aliens or copy-cat creatures.

Mum was already halfway up the stairs. Once again, Alisha found herself checking if her mother's face was the right way round. This was definitely Mum, though she seemed more serious than normal.

'You're looking at me funny,' commented Mum. 'Don't like my hairstyle?'

'Oh yeah, it's awful,' quipped Alisha.

Mum smiled at that, but only briefly. Alisha wondered what was wrong. This wasn't what it was like when Mum struggled with her big feelings – this was something else.

'Have you got your friends over?' asked Mum.

'Yeah. The Late Crew.'

'As a parent, I shouldn't approve of that name, but I quite like it. However, you'll need to ask them to go home. I've had a call from Miss Penn today.'

Alisha felt her world freeze around her. She'd waited too long to tell Mum. Now, not only did she know about the meeting, she knew that Alisha had kept it secret!

Alisha and Mum sat at the kitchen table together. The Late Crew had all left, Tyler giving Alisha a sympathetic look when she explained why they had to go.

'I was going to tell you eventually,' said Alisha.

Mum had made them both hot chocolates, like she always did when they needed to talk. They weren't as fancy as the ones from Chocohut, but they were still nice.

This was the Mum she loved – the one who made hot chocolate at any time, if it would help Alisha feel better. She almost seemed to be a different person from Mum on Bad Nights, like the night before. When her Letters were winding her up, she could be quite harsh and mean.

'It's this Monday coming. I'll need to find someone to cover my shift at the shop.' Mum sounded frustrated. 'Why didn't you tell me straight away?'

'I...' Alisha did a big shrug of her shoulders. Her head was still spinning from the surprise of Mum knowing about the meeting. She'd hated the thought of telling Mum about it, but putting it off had only made it worse.

'Miss Penn said you've been tired in school. That you were falling asleep in a lesson?'

'That's right.' Alisha stared at her legs, rather than looking at Mum. She hated talking about this.

'Have you told school why you're tired?'

Alisha shook her head. She felt tears prick the corners of her eyes. Mum had never asked to have Letters and Bad Nights, or for her daughter to have to stay up to look after her.

'You've got nothing to be ashamed of.'

'I know I don't!' Alisha burst out. 'I've *never ever* been ashamed of your Letters. I just don't want to be treated differently to everyone else at school just because you have Bad Nights sometimes. I want to be … *normal*.'

For a moment, Mum looked upset. Before working with her support lady, that comment would have been enough to set off big feelings for her. She'd have started calling herself a bad mother, and Alisha would have felt really guilty.

But Mum was able to handle things a bit better now. She took a deep breath, and Alisha knew she was doing one of her mental exercises that helped – maybe counting backwards or noticing different colours in the room.

Then Mum said: 'There's no such thing as normal. Everyone tries to fit themselves into how they think they should be. But we're all weird and different really. It's what makes us shine. And you shine so brightly, my Alisha star.'

Alisha managed a smile, though she could still feel the sad lump in her throat.

'If you tell school the truth about why you're tired, you can also tell them how you'd like to be treated. If they don't listen to you, they'll have me to answer to. And I can be scary. I'll show them big-feelings anger!'

Mum pulled an angry face, and Alisha laughed.

'You and I can make changes too. We don't always need to watch two or three whole films when I have a Bad Night. I'll tell you earlier when I'm OK and you can go to bed without worrying.'

'I don't want to make it worse for your Letters,' said Alisha.

'No ifs, no buts. I may have this gorgeous young face, but I'm still your mum. Me and my Letters will manage.'

Out of nowhere, Mum blew a big raspberry, imitating the sound of a fart. It set them both giggling. Mum couldn't stay serious for too long!

'By the way,' said Mum. 'I haven't forgotten your punishment. You didn't tell me about the after-school meeting. That's almost teenage-level misbehaving. I'm thinking … no ChocoHut trips for a month.'

'Noooooo!'

IF ONLY HUMANS SLEPT AS WELL AS CATS

Alisha lay under her covers, looking up at the pale moonlight on the ceiling. It was late now, almost eleven o'clock. Mum had gone to bed hours ago. Alisha couldn't sleep – even though she was exhausted from the day, as well as Mum's Bad Night the night before.

All she wanted to do was drift off. If she could sleep, then she could forget about Head of Year meetings and copy-cat aliens, at least for a little while. So, of course, she felt one hundred percent alert and awake. It was **infuriating!**

'I saw an alien today,' she whispered to Hugo's curled-up shape at the bottom of the bed. 'It was the copy-cat creature from last night again. It transformed into a hedgehog, a pigeon, a mouse, an owl, and, *oh yes* – into ME. Surely I deserve a proper night's kip!'

Hugo stirred a little at her words but didn't seem too concerned by Alisha's troubles with sleep. It wasn't a problem the cat would be familiar with. He napped any place, any time! In fact, he was nearly asleep now.

'I bet I yawn all day tomorrow,' Alisha complained, quietly so she wouldn't disturb the drowsy feline. 'And the teachers will go and tell Miss Penn that I'm tired again. And I could avoid it all – *if I could just go to sleep*!'

Hugo stretched, pushing his paws out along the bed. Alisha had never seen another person or animal look so perfectly relaxed.

'Show off,' she muttered.

To her surprise, Hugo lifted his head. He sniffed repeatedly, his whiskers twitching.

Alisha saw his eyes flash green, catching the light from outside. Then he began to let out a low *grrrrrowl.*

'Jeez, OK, you're not a show off.'

Hugo jumped over to her bedside table, glaring out of the window. His black hair and tail puffed up, and his *grrrooow-woowwooll* got louder and angrier.

'*Shhh,* you'll wake Mum.'

Alisha swung her legs out of bed and joined Hugo by the window. She knew what to look for – *two* of anything.

She quickly found what she was searching for. There were the shadowy shapes of two crows perched in the tree behind her house. One preened at its ruffled feathers. The other's head was turned to the side, as if it had a single eye fixed on Alisha. It might have been her imagination, but she swore she saw that beady eye glint in the moonlight.

She moved back from the glass, breathing fast. That *had* to be the copy-cat creature. Hugo retreated with her, his hair raised. He'd stopped growling at least, the last thing she needed was Mum coming in to see what the noise was!

She knew what had upset her cat. The metal scent was drifting in from the window. Hugo must have smelt it and known the alien was back.

'Why are you here?' whispered Alisha, leaning forward to peek out again. She wondered if the copy-crow could somehow hear her. 'Why is it me you're hanging around … and me you made a copy of?'

The real crow flew away, leaving the branch bobbing up and down. The copy-crow tilted its head, still staring at her.

'And what is a Difference Machine?' asked Alisha. 'What's coming here?'

She wouldn't find out any answers in her bedroom. And it was too late at night to get help from the rest of The Late Crew. There was only one thing for it. She was going to go out and face the copy-cat creature, alone!

BAD IDEAS ARE THE BEST WAY TO MEET ALIENS

'This is a bad idea,' Alisha whispered nervously to herself, as she slipped out of her bedroom in the dark. 'A *really* bad idea.'

Alisha stopped outside Mum's bedroom and listened at the door. From the slow breathing inside, Alisha could tell Mum was fast asleep. She'd done this before, on Bad Nights – when she'd wanted to make sure Mum had actually got to sleep after having big feelings.

'*Definitely* a bad idea,' Alisha muttered as she crept down the stairs, carefully avoiding the creaky centres of the steps. She gripped the bannister on the way down

– as if holding on tight would somehow stop an alien, if one decided to snatch her!

Once she reached the front door, she took out her phone and sent a quick message to The Late Crew.

The copy-cat is outside my window. It's a crow now. I'm going to try talking to it. Wish me luck ✿
– ALISHAAA

P.S. Hope I speak to the alien, and don't end up trying to talk to a real crow – ALISHAAA

Alisha walked out on to the grass behind the flat. Everything was lit by moonlight, so even the grass below her feet looked grey. It was cool outside in her pyjamas, but at least she'd put on a coat and trainers. Above her, on a bare tree branch, the dark shape of the copy-crow watched her. The smell of metal drifted down.

'Um, hi,' said Alisha.

She heard the sound of shuffling feathers, but the bird didn't respond in any other way.

'You've been following me,' she added, feeling a bit ridiculous. She didn't have any experience talking to birds. 'What do you want?'

Still no answer. She thought about Levi saying the copy-cat had run away from The Late Crew. She was terrified, out here alone in the middle of the night, speaking to a creature she was almost certain was an alien. But to the copy-cat, Alisha was the strange and scary alien.

It was the same as when people thought Mum was difficult to understand because of her Letters. But to her, *they* were the ones who were difficult to understand! Maybe she needed to treat the copy-cat creature with the kindness she wished people would show to Mum.

'I won't hurt you, I promise,' said Alisha, in a soft voice. 'I want to help. But you have to tell me how.'

The crow dropped from the tree and glided down: and **WHOOOSH** – with a quieter sound, it disappeared in silver smoke and became a sparrow. Then **WHOOOSH** it became a wren, and finally, **WHOOOSH** a robin, fluttering in front of Alisha before landing on the grass.

It was as if the creature was calmer now. Its transformations were less frantic and made less smoke. The copy-robin hopped along the grass, then stopped and looked back at Alisha. It wanted her to follow it somewhere. She sighed, glancing back towards the safety of her flat.

'I should have stayed in bed,' Alisha said, rolling her eyes, and then followed the robin anyway.

NEVER ASK A ROBIN
FOR DIRECTIONS

The copy-robin led Alisha through
Morfield, walking through streets of
houses with all their lights off. They didn't
see a single other person, and there was
only the rare sound of a car in the distance.
It felt like the rest of the town was asleep,
apart from her and the robin.

The bird never stayed still:
             fluttering from a fence post
                          to the pavement
             to a parked car's wing mirror
                          to the top of a bin
to under a streetlight.

She tried talking to the robin as they
walked, but all it did was twitter back at

her then continue on its way.

Alisha checked her phone, but none of The Late Crew had replied. They'd all be asleep. It was almost midnight, which made Alisha gulp. She'd be in so much trouble if Mum found out she was out of the house. She'd be grounded for the rest of the year – and it was only February!

They turned on to a new street, and Alisha saw the swimming pool up ahead. In the daytime, it would be busy and bustling. Now it was utterly silent. It felt eerie, like a place that had been abandoned.

Alisha suddenly realised where they were going. The copy-robin was taking her towards Morfield Woods! She sent another message to The Late Crew:

You won't see this until morning, but the copy-cat became a robin. It's taking me to Morfield Woods 🌳🌳🌳
– ALISHAAA

If I'm not in school tomorrow, it's

because it became a lion, or a big
alien monster, and ate me
– ALISHAAA

Alisha was joking, but she was genuinely
scared. She kept reminding herself of what
Levi said, that the copy-cat had actually
been frightened of *them*. If it was planning
on eating humans, it probably wouldn't
find them scary!

The copy-robin perched on the bike
gate at the back of the swimming pool.
When Alisha caught up with it, the bird
flew down the hill and landed in one of the
trees. It looked dark inside the woods, like
the setting of a creepy fairytale. It was one
thing walking through the town at night –
but this was too far!

'Nope, I'm not going in there,' she
announced as she went down the slope, her
heart hammering in her chest. 'No way.
I've followed you all the way here. I know
you can turn into a person. You do that
now, and explain to me what's going on.'

She felt silly giving the copy-robin commands, but she was not – repeat, NOT – going into those woods! The robin hopped off the branch, wings wide. As it flew down **WHOOOOSHHHH**, a silver cloud formed.

An identical pair of shoes to her own touched on to the ground. The copy-Alisha was even wearing the same pyjamas and coat she was wearing now. It would have been like looking into a mirror, if it wasn't for the dark trees of Morfield Woods behind the copy-Alisha.

'Could you become someone else?' asked Alisha. She was creeped out enough already, without staring at her own mirror image. 'It's too weird, talking to me.'

This time it was just a brief **POOF!** of smoke. The copy-cat creature became a boy, the same height as Alisha, wearing the Morfield Secondary school uniform. At a quick glance, he could be any pupil from their school.

It was only when she looked closer, that

she realised he was all of The Late Crew mixed together. He had Tyler's sticky up hair, and Grace's eyes. His face was like Jayden's, but also like Levi's. His eyebrows, strangely, were copies of Alisha's own.

'Well, that's better, I guess,' said Alisha. She hadn't expected that! 'Can you speak English?'

'I learnt from you,' the copy-cat said. His voice sounded a bit like Grace's, and a bit like Jayden's. Alisha didn't know how the creature could have possibly learnt their language so quickly.

'Well, you know my name,' said Alisha. 'What should I call you?'

His face, a mixture of herself and her friends, was pale in the moonlight. 'I am Xzorysssnoripipoxitizxyxl.'

'Erm,' said Alisha, unsure how to repeat that. 'What if I just call you Copy?'

'That would be fine.'

'Well, Copy,' said Alisha. 'Would you mind telling me who you are? And why you've been following me?'

The wind blew, and the trees swayed behind the alien. His expression was calm, and perhaps a little sad. He was a stranger. Yet because of how he'd copied The Late Crew, he looked so familiar to her. Almost like when she knew she'd met someone before but couldn't remember from where or when.

'Of course,' said Copy. 'I'll tell you my story, Alisha from Earth.'

COPY'S STORY

'I'm from a planet called Xoxorathia-Zarapa-Vee,' said Copy. 'It's a beautiful place. We have purple grass, and orange seas that glitter when our two suns rise. On Xoxorathia-Zarapa-Vee – '

We might need to think of a shorter name for that too, Alisha thought to herself, but didn't interrupt.

' – we live in family pods. In my pod, it was my father-parent, my mother-parent and me. On the day everything changed, we were having a celebration, as our planet had travelled round the sun eleven times since I was born.'

'Wait,' said Alisha. She thought she understood what he was describing. 'You're talking about celebrating your eleventh birthday? With your mum and dad?'

'That's right. Though our years are shorter than yours. In Earth years, I'm about ten and a half.'

'Wow,' said Alisha. She couldn't believe that Copy was younger than her!

'Our species look like yours – except we have blue skin and are much smaller. That's what I looked like, until my birthday. That morning, I was in my room, thinking about the gifts I'd soon open. I started to feel strange, like my *entire body* needed to sneeze. I felt a bubbling under my skin and got really, really warm. Suddenly, silver smoke shot out of me like a big *achoo*, and I morphed into a copy of my pet ten-legged lizard!'

Who would have guessed an alien would know what a sneeze was? His species must sneeze too! Alisha thought. But she knew that wasn't the most important question to ask right now.

'So you'd never transformed before? And then you became your pet on your birthday?' she asked, imagining unexpectedly transforming into Hugo. It must have been very confusing.

'That was the first time,' said Copy. 'I managed to turn back before my parents saw. The next day, I got the feeling again at school-pod. I said I needed the waste-flush-room. I hid in there, trying not to transform into anything. But I could hear little birds called fourwings singing outside. Next thing I knew, I became one.'

'Can I ask a question?' asked Alisha.

'I believe you just did,' replied Copy, and for a moment his voice sounded like Alisha's.

Alisha snorted. Of course, he copied her voice to say something sassy.

'Well, another question then. Why did you hide your power? If I could turn into animals, I'd spend the whole day showing off!'

Copy looked at his shoes. Something about the way he hunched his shoulders made Alisha feel sorry for him.

'Shapeshifters are rare on my planet,' he said, in a small voice. 'Every so often someone's born that way. They find out what they are when they grow up. People don't like them.'

'Why not?' asked Alisha. It sounded really unfair, judging someone for something they couldn't even help.

'Shapeshifters are seen as creepy, or liars,' said Copy. 'Because they can pretend to be other people. Imagine speaking to your friend, and telling them all your secrets – and then realising you were speaking to a shapeshifter all along.'

'But that's not right!' protested Alisha. It reminded her of how people spoke about Mum. 'Yeah, a shapeshifter could pretend to be someone else. It doesn't mean they actually would do it! Anyone *could* do something bad or sneaky, if they wanted to.'

Copy shrugged, as if to say *that's just how it is*. Alisha thought he must be feeling very lonely, standing by the woods on a cold night, on a planet that wasn't his own.

'I kept transforming more and more,' said Copy. 'Until I knew there was no way

I'd be able to keep my secret any longer. I couldn't bear for my parents to find out that I was a shapeshifter. So I stole our family's spaceship and flew away. I picked up your beacon, for aliens that need help… and that's how I've ended up here.'

Alisha thought it was horrible. Copy hadn't done anything wrong. But because he'd discovered he was a shapeshifter, he felt so awful about himself that he'd run away from home rather than face his parents knowing the truth.

'Are you sure your, uh, mother-parent and father-parent would have such a bad reaction if they found out?' said Alisha. 'Maybe they'd surprise you.'

Copy did another one of his shrugs. 'I just know they don't like shapeshifters. And I haven't even told you the worst part.'

'What's the worst part?' asked Alisha, with a sinking feeling in her stomach.

'Someone on my planet must know my secret already. They've reported me – and sent a Difference Machine after me.'

THE DIFFERENCE MACHINE

'A Difference Machine?' repeated Alisha. There was something about the phrase that made her shiver, and remember she was out after dark. She looked fearfully into the shadows in Morfield Woods. 'You mentioned that on the grass, by my flat. You said one was coming.'

'That's right. I saw it on my spaceship's scanners, following me from Xoxorathia-Zarapa-Vee. It'll be here in four of your days.'

'I'm sorry,' said Alisha. 'But what *is* a Difference Machine?'

'It's the robot used to arrest shapeshifters.'

'What do you mean *arrest*?' asked Alisha. 'Don't you have to have broken a law to be arrested? Is being a shapeshifter against the law?'

'No, it's not,' explained Copy. 'But it's against our laws for shapeshifters to transform.'

'But you said you can't always control when you transform! That's not right!' Alisha was almost shouting. She felt like her whole body was burning with frustration at the unfairness of it all.

Copy just shook his head. He reminded Alisha of a half-deflated balloon. She imagined before his birthday, he'd been a happy and energetic alien kid. Then he'd found out he was a shapeshifter, and nothing had been the same since.

'Why did you bring me here?' asked Alisha quietly. Copy didn't seem like a threat at all. But after hearing about the Difference Machine, the edge of Morfield Woods at night suddenly felt like a very creepy place to be.

'I got your message, from the beacon in the woods. I came to you because it said

The Late Crew help aliens in need,' said Copy. Then he added nervously, 'But I wanted to speak here because my spaceship is nearby. People have such bad reactions to shapeshifters on my planet ... I thought it might be the same on Earth. I wanted to be able to escape, if I needed to.'

Levi had been right. Copy really was as afraid of them as they were of him. He'd even made an escape plan to get away from her if he needed to!

'We do help aliens in need,' Alisha said reassuringly, trying to make Copy feel less frightened. She decided not to mention that they'd only helped aliens once before! 'But what can we do? How can we stop the Difference Machine?'

A helpless expression appeared on Copy's face. It was strange, because the more time she spent with Copy, the more she forgot he looked like The Late Crew all mixed together. Instead, it was just like talking to a new pupil at her school. But in that moment, she saw her friends and herself in him – all looking frightened.

'Everyone says nothing can stop a Difference Machine,' said Copy. 'I don't even properly know what one looks like. I've heard they have a single glowing red eye, and you can *feel* when one is watching you. Their red eye scans for anything different to what it's supposed to be. It's how they find shapeshifters.'

'So if we want to hide you from it...' Alisha began.

'Then you have to teach me how to fit in perfectly on Earth. By the day you call Monday.'

'So plenty of time to teach you about an entire planet,' she quipped, hiding her fear with sarcasm. Teaching an alien to blend in on Earth sounded hard enough already, without a four-day time limit!

'That's *still* not the worst part,' Copy added glumly.

Alisha raised her eyebrows. How many worst parts could there be?

'If someone asks for a Difference

Machine to follow you, that means they suspect you're a shapeshifter and want you to be arrested. This one was called almost as soon as I left the planet with my parents' ship. I think maybe...' Copy paused, as if what he was thinking was too terrible to say aloud. 'I think maybe it was my parents who sent the Difference Machine after me.'

Copy let out a long and tired sigh. Alisha couldn't imagine how he must be feeling. There'd been times when Mum had been too unwell with her Letters to be able to properly look after Alisha – but she'd always *wanted* to be there for her. She'd certainly never send a robot after her own child!

'My friends and I are going to find a way to help you,' said Alisha, hoping she sounded more confident than she felt. 'Helping aliens is what we do. But first, I have a LOT of questions.'

ALISHA INTERVIEWS AN ALIEN

Can you control when you change?

'If I want to, I can make myself change and choose what I change into. But sometimes I start feeling weird, and can't stop myself. It happens when I'm feeling a strong emotion too. For example, I was panicking when you were chasing me around the grass – I didn't mean to keep changing!'

Can you become anything you want?

'It has to be a real animal, and it's easier if the creature I'm copying is nearby. I can only imitate what I've seen, not make something new up. But I can mix things together, like how I've made myself into a mix of you and your friends.'

What's it like when you transform?

'I'm still me, but I take on a bit of the personality of whatever I become. So when I was the mouse, I felt very little and afraid. When I was your cat, I felt more adventurous. It's strange, seeing the world through their eyes.'

Can I see what you look like normally?

'I haven't been able to change back into myself since I ran away. I don't know why. I really want to be back in my own body.'

Can you show me your spaceship?

Rather than answering the question directly, Copy headed into Morfield Woods, then moments later reappeared carrying a black rock about the size of a beach ball. It looked like a meteorite, with a lumpy not-quite-round shape and loads of holes in it.

'That's your spaceship?' Alisha exclaimed in surprise.

'Yes, it is.'

Copy placed it down on the ground between them. Alisha looked at the holes in the rock. A mouse could get in, and maybe a hedgehog could squeeze its way into one of the bigger gaps. Hugo definitely wouldn't fit!

'You weren't kidding when you said your species are small!' said Alisha.

'I'd say you're all big,' replied Copy, and Alisha heard her own sass in his voice again. She wasn't sure she liked it when someone did it back to her!

'Couldn't you just fly away, before the Difference Machine gets here?'

'I had a head start, but the Difference Machine is faster than my spaceship. There's no way I can outrun it. That's why I need to hide.'

Alisha had asked all her questions – apart from the one that she *had* to know the answer to: 'Why is it me you've been watching? Couldn't you have followed any of The Late Crew?'.

'After I found your beacon, I did watch each member of your group – but it was *you* that I realised would be able to help. You can help me act human, so no one knows I'm not from Earth.'

'Why would I be able to do that more than anyone else?' asked Alisha.

'Because you lie and pretend to fit in, like I'll have to.'

'Oi!' said Alisha, offended. 'I don't lie and pretend!'

Copy looked shocked by her reaction, and his face flushed red.

'I didn't mean to insult you,' the alien boy said hurriedly. He seemed like he wasn't sure how to explain himself. 'I only meant … you misled your teacher, Miss Penn, about why you were tired in school. Because you wanted her to see you as a 🎵 *very normal perfectly proper girl.* 🎵'

He said the last part in an exact copy of Alisha's singsong voice.

'And you told your classmates that you were in trouble for making too many jokes,' Copy continued. 'Which wasn't true. You were hiding the fact that your life at home is different to theirs.'

'Alright, fine!' replied Alisha grumpily. 'You've made your point.'

Copy looked at her helplessly, like he knew he'd upset her but didn't understand why. It wasn't the alien's fault. The annoying thing was, he was right!

Alisha did lie, all the time. Because she didn't want people to treat her or Mum unfairly if they found out how she helped Mum with her Letters. And now Copy had to lie and pretend too, because shapeshifters were treated so horribly where he was from.

'You're not alone on this planet,' Alisha told the alien boy. 'I'm going to introduce you to my friends. And we're not going to let any stinking Difference Machine take you away.'

HUMANS ARE JUST BIG HOT WATER BOTTLES FOR CATS

'It's getting very late,' said Alisha, and yawned. 'I need to get some sleep.'

It was almost half-past midnight and hearing Copy's story had tired her out. He must have been even more exhausted from answering all her questions! She agreed with her new alien friend that The Late Crew would meet him here tomorrow, after school.

The idea of leaving Copy alone in Morefield Woods worried her, but he insisted that he'd be fine. After he'd carried his meteor spaceship into the woods and hidden it again, the alien transformed into a fox. Alisha watched his red and white tail as he slunk away between the trees.

She had to admit that Copy was right – he'd have no problem spending a night in the forest as a fox. He'd be a lot better off than her if Mum caught her coming home this late!

Alisha climbed the stairs in the dark. She was relieved to find no signs of Mum having woken up while she was out. The lights were all off, and it was quiet. Everything was exactly as she'd left it.

However, somebody did notice her coming in late. Hugo circled excitedly around her legs, almost tripping her as she tiptoed into her bedroom.

'Hey, watch it,' murmured Alisha, careful not to speak loudly enough for Mum to hear. 'You're going to get me in trouble.'

She bent down and stroked Hugo, listening intently for any movement from Mum's room. If she woke up now, Alisha would need to attempt to explain the fact she had her coat and shoes on! Luckily, there was no sound – other than the cat's increasingly happy purring.

Alisha took her coat and shoes off, moving slowly to stay quiet. When she finally got into bed, Hugo jumped up and got comfortable on top of the covers.

'So that's why you were happy to see me,' whispered Alisha. 'You wanted me to make the bed warm.'

Hugo made a satisfied *prrrrp* sound, which Alisha took to mean yes. She gazed out of the window as the cat drifted to sleep. Above the tree outside, she could see twinkling stars. Each star was a burning sun, just like their own. They only looked small because they were far away.

It made her feel funny to imagine so many suns – especially as Levi had told her that scientists thought most of them had their own planets spinning around them! Somewhere out there, orbiting a distant star, was Copy's planet.

There were scientists whose job it was

to find new planets, and search for signs of life. Clearly none of them had found Xoxorathia-Zarapa-Vee yet! Alisha was surprised she remembered its bizarre name. Then again, she was the first human on Earth to know about the planet, and the aliens who lived on it.

Xoxorathia-Zarapa-Vee, with its glittering orange seas and small blue aliens who went to school in pods. It was a place where people were treated unfairly for being different. Just like Earth. It was sad to think that even out there in space, that was the way things were.

She *had* to find a way of helping Copy. She couldn't let the Difference Machine capture him and put him in an alien prison. Even if she didn't know:

- What the Difference Machine looked like
- How they'd teach Copy to hide from it
- Or how they'd make it leave once it arrived on Earth!

Which, admittedly, was rather a lot not to know. But one thing was certain. Whatever the plan was, she was going to need The Late Crew by her side!

THE ON-TIME CREW JUST DOESN'T HAVE THE SAME RING TO IT

'So, Copy wants us to teach him how to fit in on Earth?' asked Tyler.

'That's right,' said Alisha.

It was breaktime the next day. Alisha, Tyler, Grace and Jayden had gathered by the fence next to the astroturf, speaking in low voices. The only member of The Late Crew missing was Levi, who was at his primary school.

They'd picked this spot because there was no one nearby to overhear them talking about aliens. The closest other pupils were a group of Year 8 girls having a kickabout in the five-a-side nets. Those girls played football every breaktime and lunchtime – Alisha was surprised they hadn't worked out a way to fit in quick games in the corridors between lessons.

'His story is so sad,' said Grace. 'He couldn't even tell his parents about his new powers. They must really not like shapeshifters on his planet.'

'Everyone said to him you can't trust shapeshifters,' said Jayden, unusually serious. 'And then he found out he was one. That's rough.'

'It's *prejudice*,' said Grace. There was a frustrated growl in her voice, like Alisha's anger at the injustice of it all the night before. It was surprising, coming from Grace, who was usually so gentle. 'That's what it's called, when people assume bad things about you just because you're different to them. And if you hear everyone else saying how awful you are, you can start believing it about yourself.'

Alisha nodded. It was like the assumptions people made about Mum because of her Letters. Like thinking she couldn't have a job, or be good at being a parent. Mum used to get really down on herself because of that. Having her support lady and going to her group had helped her realise that what people assumed about her wasn't true.

Maybe that was the worst bit for Copy. Every mean thing he'd been taught about shapeshifters, he'd think about himself now.

After break, Alisha and Tyler had Geography together, on the second floor. As they went up the stairs, Tyler told her that he and Levi had been discussing how Copy's transformations might work. He spoke like it was all a sci-fi story he was making up, in case anyone around them was listening in.

Tyler was halfway through explaining his brother's theory that Copy became like Play-Doh inside the silver smoke, when Alisha saw Miss Penn descending towards them. The Head of Year was telling some boys off for messing around and hadn't noticed her yet.

Miss Penn would definitely want to talk about calling Mum and finding out that Alisha hadn't passed on the message about the meeting. She'd probably even bring it up right there, even though most of Alisha's Geography class were on the stairs!

Alisha turned and followed a group of older girls into a first-floor hallway, acting completely natural, as if that was the way she'd meant to walk in the first place.

'Have you forgotten where the Geography rooms are?' asked Tyler behind her, smirking a little.

He'd followed her when she turned off the wrong way. Alisha glanced at the door to the stairway, which had a little round glass window in it. Miss Penn passed by without looking in their direction.

'Well, a map would help,' Alisha quipped. 'But unfortunately, all the maps are in the geography room, so I'm stuck.'

'Why are you avoiding Miss Penn?'

Alisha hesitated, unsure how much to tell Tyler. She'd mentioned her meetings with Miss Penn to him before, but she hadn't actually told him why she had them.

He was a young carer too, so it'd all make sense to him. And he called Miss Penn *The One Who Doesn't Understand*, so he probably had experience of trying to stay out of her way as well!

Copy was right last night – when Alisha was at school, she did hide the truth about her life. But if there was anyone she could trust enough to be honest with, it was Tyler.

'Mum and I have a meeting with her after school on Monday,' explained Alisha. 'Because I've been tired in lessons, from looking after Mum at night. I didn't want Miss Penn to talk about the meeting on the stairs, where everybody would listen.'

'Been there,' said Tyler, with a knowing expression. 'The meeting's meant to be private, but then a teacher shouts to you across the hallway about it. Also, they say you're not in trouble, but it sounds a bit like you are the whole time.'

'Yes!' said Alisha, pleased someone else had noticed teachers did that. 'They say they want to *support* you, and make sure you're *reaching your potential...*'

'And that they want you to *be able to focus in lessons...*' added Tyler.

'So you aren't *distracted* or *struggling to concentrate...*' continued Alisha.

'Which all sounds sort of fine...'

'Except it's exactly what they say when you're getting told off too!'

They both laughed. Alisha felt better knowing she wasn't the only one who teachers spoke to in that weird way.

'We better get to Geography,' said Tyler. 'Getting told off for being late won't help anything.'

The two of them hurried towards their lesson. The stairs were nearly empty, most people already in their classrooms, but as long as they were fast, they'd avoid being in too much trouble.

'We'll have to explain that we're part of The Late Crew. We can't start being on time for stuff.' Alisha winked at Tyler. 'We'd have to change our name!'

ALIENS WITHOUT TENTACLES ARE EASIER TO SHAKE HANDS WITH

The entire Late Crew – including Levi now – walked down the path to Morfield Woods. It was the evening, and the sun was setting. The clouds and sky were red and purple colours like a painting, and the trees were casting long shadows.

Alisha hoped Copy would meet them there, like he'd said he would. She would feel almost like she dreamt the events of the night before if he didn't turn up. And what would they do next, if he was gone?

But sure enough, a single tree branch was weighed down by two sparrows. One bird flew down towards them and

WHOOOOSH became Copy, standing on the grass. Tyler, Levi, Grace and Jayden stared wide-eyed at the alien in his human form. Alisha wondered how Copy's hours alone in the forest had been, and what animals he'd become through the night.

'Hello, everyone,' said Copy. 'Thank you for meeting me.'

'Does he ... sound like me?' asked Jayden. He normally acted tough, but even he was unnerved by seeing a boy who was a mixture of The Late Crew all together.

'You and Grace, I think,' said Alisha.

'Ugh,' groaned Grace. 'I hate hearing my own voice. Like on recordings and stuff.'

'Is that my hair?' asked Tyler. 'Is it really that messy?'

'It is,' confirmed Alisha, with a cheeky grin. 'But we'll get you a comb for your birthday.'

Levi stepped forward from the rest of The Late Crew and held his hand out. Copy looked down at the outstretched hand, utter confusion on his face.

'You shake it,' explained Levi. 'It's a way we say hello on Earth.'

Alisha spotted Tyler nodding proudly. Levi must have thought ahead about the best way to introduce himself to a visitor from another world. Copy took Levi's hand, then swung it wildly from side to side. Levi looked shocked and took a deep, trembling breath when the alien let go of his hand.

Alisha knew that Levi found certain sensations difficult because he was autistic, and he definitely wouldn't have liked having his hand pulled about like that! But he'd tried not to react to the alien's mistake. He was so determined to help Copy feel comfortable on Earth.

'Thank you for the shakehand, Levi,' said Copy. He then went to each member of The Late Crew and did the same thing again, swinging their hands back and forth. They followed Levi's lead and didn't make a big deal out of him not doing it right.

We'll need to teach him the correct way

eventually, if he's going to fit in on Earth, Alisha thought. *But how would any of us feel, trying something for the first time and immediately being told we were doing it wrong?*

'You have taught me an Earth custom,' said Copy. 'Does this mean you'll help me to hide myself on this planet?'

'We'll help you,' replied Alisha, and the rest of The Late Crew nodded.

'Thank you,' said Copy. He seemed relieved, like he hadn't been sure they would all agree to it. 'I'm grateful for your assistance.'

'I just wondered...' asked Grace, uncertainly. 'Do you want us to tell more people about you? Because we could ask an adult for help.'

Alisha looked at Grace in surprise. She'd been so used to The Late Crew keeping their alien encounters secret, she hadn't even thought that they could tell someone if they wanted to. The adults would have to believe them as well – they had an actual alien as proof!

'Please don't tell anyone else about me,' said Copy, sounding worried. 'You five have met aliens before. But if someone new meets an alien for the very first time, they'll definitely act strangely – and draw the Difference Machine towards us!'

That made sense to Alisha. Especially when it came to telling adults. Most of them couldn't deal with anything a little bit out of the ordinary, let alone aliens. Though Alisha did think Mum would probably take an alien arriving in her stride – even if one landed a big spaceship on the roof of their flat!

'There's one huge issue,' said Jayden, finding the problem as always. 'It's Friday today, and we need to teach Copy how to be a human by Monday. How are we supposed to do that over one weekend?'

THE HUMAN RULEBOOK IS 1,437 PAGES LONG

The Late Crew and Copy all looked at each other, but no one had the answer. Jayden had raised a good point. How *did* you teach someone to be human?

'Wouldn't it be easier to turn into a bird or mouse when the Difference Machine arrives?' asked Alisha. 'Humans are a bit … complicated.'

That's the understatement of the year, thought Alisha. *Humans are **very** complicated!*

'The Difference Machine would find me immediately if I became an animal,' explained Copy. 'A bird can't tell me how to be a bird. If I even flapped my wings at the wrong time, the Machine would know. Because humans are more "complicated", there's more differences between them anyway – so it's harder for the Machine to detect me.'

'Why's it never easy?' complained Jayden, with an exasperated sigh. 'It's not like there's a set of rules about how to be a person.'

'There sort of is,' interjected Levi.

'Like the handshake?' said Tyler, looking thoughtful.

'Yes,' answered his younger brother. 'The rule is that if someone puts their hand out, you shake it to say hello. If you didn't know the rule, you wouldn't know what to do in that situation.'

'Have you thought of any others?' asked Grace.

'There are loads. I think I notice them more, because I'm autistic,' said Levi, before counting off some examples on his fingers:

THUMB 'People want you to look into their eyes when they're talking, even if you don't like making eye contact.'

FIRST FINGER 'People can laugh in a funny "ha-ha" way, or a mean making-fun-of-you way, and you have to know which is which.'

SECOND FINGER 'When someone says something like "it's raining cats and dogs", you don't look around for the cats and dogs. Because it's an expression, and they're not really there.'

Alisha took a deep breath. Levi was right. There were *so many* rules to follow to fit in as a human. She'd learnt them without even knowing. But what hope did they have of thinking of all the rules, and teaching them to Copy, over one weekend?

Then Alisha had a brainwave. None of them had sat down and studied a book called The Rules of Humans. They'd learnt by living and being around people. Copy needed to do that too.

'We need to get you out and about, meeting people,' said Alisha. 'You need to practise being a human. Then we can tell you when you make a mistake.'

'That's a good plan,' agreed Grace. 'Even if we're not able to think up all the different rules we follow, we'll know what's right or wrong when we actually see it.'

'That seems smart,' said Tyler, and Levi nodded too.

'I'll try that,' said Copy, not quite managing to keep a nervous tremble out of his voice. Being around lots of humans was going to be a challenge for the alien!

Everyone turned to Jayden, waiting for his opinion.

'Let's give it a go,' he said, with a shrug. 'There's only about a thousand ways it could go wrong.'

GREETINGS FROM PLANET CANADA

When it started to get dark, The Late Crew split up and went home. Copy went with Tyler and Levi, to sleep over at their house. Sleeping in the woods wasn't a good way to practise normal human behaviour! He was going to stay at Grace's the next night, then Jayden's the one after – though Jayden said it'd be a squeeze with all his brothers and sisters!

Alisha was jealous. She was the one who'd first met Copy, and really it was *her* flat he should have stayed in first. But with Mum's Letters, she couldn't have sleepovers there, or stay over at friend's houses. Because she never knew when Mum was going to have a Bad Night.

However, that evening, Mum actually

ended up being perfectly happy. They had oven pizzas for tea, which they ate while playing card games. It was so annoying when she chose not to do something because of Mum's Letters, but Mum ended up having a Good Night anyway. Copy could have come to theirs, and everything would have been fine!

At least on Good Nights, I know she's OK, Alisha reminded herself.

'Thinking deep thoughts?' asked Mum, her mouth full of pizza.

'Chew, then speak!' protested Alisha.

Mum obediently chewed and swallowed, then asked again, 'What were you thinking?'

'Tyler and Levi have an exchange student visiting,' said Alisha, using the story The Late Crew had come up with. 'We wanted to show him around this weekend, so he can see what things are like in the UK. Could you take us out tomorrow?'

'Sure,' said Mum, shuffling the deck of cards. 'Where's he from?'

Alisha panicked. They hadn't decided where Copy was supposed to be from!

'Um. He's from Canada.'

'Canada?' questioned Mum. 'Well, we can show him around, but I'm not sure things will be much different here than he's used to at home! What's his name?'

'Er, Cop,' said Alisha. It sounded more like a name without the y. 'He's called Cop.'

'Cop from Canada?' asked Mum. 'Well, OK then. We'll show him the best of Morfield!'

It would be a good test to see if Copy could convince Mum he was a proper human. Hopefully Copy wouldn't give himself away, but if he did, Alisha thought Mum would help keep their secret. And Mum already acted strangely, so maybe the Difference Machine wouldn't pick up anything different even if she *did* realise she'd met an alien!

And if Copy couldn't get Mum to believe he was human – what chance would he have against the Difference Machine?

THE PRETEND-TO-BE-A-HUMAN TEST

Time: Saturday 10:30 a.m.
Location: Alisha's House

Alisha answered the door when Tyler, Levi and Copy arrived. They'd originally planned to meet earlier, but Tyler had messaged to say that Levi's morning routines had taken longer than usual with Copy there too. Alisha brought the three of them upstairs to say hello to Mum.

'You have a lovely house,' said Copy, and shook Mum's hand. He did it properly this time. Tyler and Levi beamed proudly. They must have been teaching Copy manners last night!

'Well, thank you,' said Mum. 'You're much more polite than Alisha.'

Alisha stuck out her tongue.

'Point proven!' laughed Mum, before sticking hers out in response.

Copy stuck his tongue out too, and left it out, but looked unsure why everyone was doing it.

'Don't take our bad habits back to Canada, Cop!' joked Mum.

Tyler nudged Copy, who put his tongue back in his mouth. Alisha, Tyler and Levi exchanged a look as they all headed out to the car. The alien was a very long way from fitting in on Earth.

Time: Saturday 11:00 a.m.
Location: ChocoHut

When they went into Chocohut, Copy walked around and shook every person in the cafe's hand.

'I'd heard people were polite in Canada, but I never knew they were this polite!' exclaimed Mum, astonished.

'We don't normally shake *everyone's*

hand,' Alisha whispered to the alien as they sat down. 'Just if it's a new person we're being introduced to.'

Grace and Jayden arrived and sat down with them at a big table. They ordered their drinks, and Mum told Alisha she was allowed one hot chocolate as it was a special occasion with Cop visiting, but the ban was back on from then!

Grace, Levi, Copy and Mum had hot chocolates too, and Tyler had an Earl Grey tea. Copy seemed to really enjoy the hot chocolate, based on his beaming smile every time he took a sip.

Jayden ordered a coffee, insisting that his parents let him have coffee whenever he wanted. From the disgusted face he pulled when he took his first sip, Alisha knew he was lying!

Time: Saturday 11:45 a.m.
Location: Morfield Main Street
Corner Shop

Everyone picked out a sandwich, drink and crisps for lunch. It went pretty well apart from Copy trying to walk out of the shop without paying.

'Oi, that's not free you know!' growled the shopkeeper.

'Sorry, he's from Canada!' yelled Alisha, running back to pay.

As they left, the shopkeeper looked absolutely perplexed, as if he was still trying to work out why someone from Canada wouldn't know how shops worked.

Time: Saturday 12:30 p.m.
Location: The Bowling Alley

Mum got a strike with her second bowl, turning and shooting finger guns at Alisha in celebration. Copy, who'd been watching her closely, then got strikes with his next three bowls in a row!

'Humans can't do it perfectly every time,' Levi told the alien, while Mum was

bowling again. Copy seemed surprised
by that. But when it was next his turn, he
rolled his ball straight into the gutter.

'Well done – on missing!' Alisha
whispered to him.

'I copied Jayden,' replied Copy, matter-
of-factly.

Jayden, who'd kept bowling it into the
gutter, scowled. Then he shrugged his
shoulders. 'At least my misses are helping.'

Time: Saturday 1:45 p.m.
Location: Bowling Alley Car Park

None of The Late Crew wanted to leave
the bowling alley so early. They hadn't
had a chance to try a Laser Tournament
Deathmatch or play air hockey!

But being young carers meant they had
things they needed to do at weekends. Tyler
was taking Levi home then going grocery
shopping for their mum, Grace was visiting
her uncle that she helped look after, and
Jayden was making food for his younger

siblings before taking them to watch his big sister's wheelchair basketball game.

In a way, the test was a success. Mum definitely thought Copy was a bit strange, but she didn't suspect he was an alien! The problem was, Alisha doubted the alien boy was acting human enough to fool the Difference Machine. And now they only had one full day left before it arrived.

WARNING: A ROBOT IS APPROACHING THE EARTH

Time: Sunday 11:30 a.m.
Location: Grace's Bedroom

They all met at Grace's house on Sunday. She'd had the bright idea that Copy should practise being a human pupil in school. If the Difference Machine arrived tomorrow, as Copy predicted, there was a good chance they'd all be in school when it did. So the best and least "different" place for Copy to hide, would be at school too!

Of course, this being Grace, everything was extremely organised. She'd planned out parts of the day for Copy to learn about – like *how to answer the register, what to do when a teacher sets a task in class, how to respond if other pupils ask questions.*

She'd even prepared a school bag and notebooks for Copy to use, and made up a clever plan of how to get him accepted into school that day. Alisha had to admit, Grace had thought of everything!

'So, like, tell me all about your family?' chirped Jayden, doing a surprisingly good impression of Patsy, the gossip from Alisha's science class.

'I don't have brothers or sisters,' Copy replied. 'It's me, my mother-parent … sorry – my mum. And my dad. And our cat.'

It was Alisha's idea to add in the cat. Copy was getting better at being human. He was learning what to say, and what *not* to say. But he still got mixed up, and it'd be even harder at school when he didn't know what people were going to ask him in advance.

All The Late Crew could do was hope the plan worked, and that they could keep him hidden when the Difference Machine arrived.

Time: Sunday 9:30 p.m.
Location: Alisha's Front Room

Mum had a Bad Night again. She broke a cup, not even by accident, but by throwing it at the floor because she felt so wound up. Afterwards, she realised she'd upset Alisha and burst into tears.

It felt silly, but Alisha was actually quite annoyed because it was a cup she liked, with a funny picture of a cat sitting on clean washing. Sometimes it was hard, being annoyed at Mum about something her Letters had caused her to do. It felt unfair on Mum – but at the same time, she was the one who'd lost her favourite cup, which wasn't fair either.

To help Mum feel better, they watched *Love is in the Air-oplane,* a romantic comedy about strangers falling for each other during a long flight after initially not getting along at all!

Alisha thought it was probably going to be another really late night, and they'd end up watching another film to keep Mum calm. But with half an hour of their high flying rom-com left, Mum pressed pause and said she was feeling alright to go to bed.

'Are you sure?' asked Alisha. 'We can stay up longer if you need to.'

'I'm sure-sure,' said Mum, smiling as she repeated the word. 'We said we'd try to get to bed earlier, and I'm doing OK now.'

Even though it was for the best, Alisha had to admit she was a bit disappointed not to watch the rest of the film that night. She was definitely going to insist that they watched the ending soon!

Time: Sunday 10:30 p.m.
Location: Alisha's Bedroom

Alisha lay in bed, in a weird position because her legs were bent around Hugo. Despite Mum going to bed early, Alisha still couldn't sleep yet, which was irritating. She stared out of her window at the night sky, unable to stop the thoughts racing through her mind.

Will we see the Difference Machine tomorrow, and what will it look like if we do? Will it be like a robot from an old TV show, with a square head and buttons on its front? Or like a drone, buzzing around over the Earth? Will it be small, like Copy said his species were, or something huge that towers over us?

A streak of white light shot across the stars, then disappeared from sight. Surely it couldn't be... She got her phone out and messaged The Late Crew chat.

Just seen a light shoot across the sky 😁😁😁 – ALISHAAA

Levi saw it too. We couldn't sleep so he was stargazing – TY/LER

I was actually sleeping. Thanks for making my phone buzz 😑 – JAY G

@JAY G You should've put it on silent! – ALISHAAA

Copy says that was it. It's on course to arrive tomorrow – GRACE_FUL

The Difference Machine is coming 😨 – GRACE_FUL

IT IS FROWNED UPON TO PRETEND TO BE A CHICKEN AT THE OPERA

'You OK, Alisha?' asked Mum on Monday morning.

Alisha had been pushing her cornflakes around her bowl, thinking about how much fun the weekend had been with Copy – and worrying about what would happen that day. What if the Difference Machine took him away? Even Hugo seemed to know she was feeling sad and was rubbing himself against her legs under the table.

'Yeah, I'm alright,' she replied, though she knew she didn't sound very convincing. 'It was good getting to bed earlier last night.'

'I thought I did very well at not staying up late,' said Mum, putting on a smug voice. 'Well done me.'

Alisha managed a small smile, but still felt glum. At school, she'd have just pretended to be happy. But it was harder to pretend with Mum.

'Are you thinking about our meeting with Miss Penn?' asked Mum, looking concerned. 'Remember, I'm on your side, and no one messes with me.'

Actually, Alisha had completely forgotten about their after-school meeting today. It didn't seem very important compared to being chased across the universe by a difference-detecting robot!

'It won't be too awful,' said Alisha, with a tired sigh. 'Miss Penn's a bit stuffy, and cares *way too much* about having your shirt tucked in, but at least she's trying to help. I just wish she'd leave me alone to get on with it. She won't understand what our life's like.'

'Well, maybe you can explain it to her.'

'*Meeeeeehhh.*'

'What?' laughed Mum.

'You're being so ... reasonable. It's not like you. I don't like it.' Alisha said, with a grin to show she wasn't serious.

'Ah, that's because I'm a *confident person*, who's learnt how to *manage my feelings*.' Mum winked, because she was using the words her support lady did. 'I'm a very grown-up, prim and proper mother now. I'm going to take you to the opera, and teach you about fine dining with silver knives and forks.'

'I hope not,' groaned Alisha.

'Well, either that or I'll take you back to the ChocoHut once your ban runs out. We'll see.'

Hugo meowed from under the table and Alisha went to the cat food cupboard. She opened a packet that smelt strongly of fish, and squeezed it out into his bowl for him. The cat munched away happily.

'You support me,' said Mum gratefully. 'And look after Hugo too. At least I don't bring in birds! I don't know what's going on with your friend Cop from Canada, but I could tell you were taking care of him as well. You deserve to be proud of who you are. If school or anyone else has a problem with it – then that's their problem, not yours!'

'You're doing the reasonable thing again!'

'Would it help if I did something ridiculous?'

Alisha nodded. Mum did her very best impression of a chicken, strutting around the room and *bu-cawwww-ing*. She liked what Mum had said, about being proud. But what about Copy? Why couldn't he be proud of who he was too? Why did he have to hide on another planet, hunted by a machine, just because he was different?

The Difference Machine sounded really scary. Alisha was dreading the fact she might meet it that day. But if she *did* see the robot – she'd make certain to let it know it wasn't welcome on planet Earth!

THE SUPER-SECRET-GET-COPY-ACCEPTED-TO-SCHOOL PLAN

Later that morning, Alisha and Jayden walked into the school reception with someone who looked very much like Mr Hail. But it wasn't the tall, serious headteacher. Copy had become the head's mirror image, even down to his smart blue suit.

'It's important we don't let the real Mr Hail see you,' Alisha whispered to the copy-headteacher. 'Because last term he had his brain taken over by alien slime. I don't think he fully remembers what happened, but I'm not sure he could take any more weirdness.'

Mr Cuthbert was at the reception desk. He stared over his glasses towards them, a nosy expression on his face. He was clearly wondering why Alisha and Jayden were standing with the headteacher.

'Now, tell him what we practised,' Alisha said, in a low voice.

'*Exactly* what we practised,' added Jayden.

The copy-headteacher nodded, then walked up to the reception desk.

'Mr Cuthbert, Jayden Green has an exchange student named Cop staying with him this week,' the copy-headteacher said. 'Please let the teachers know that he'll be attending Jayden's classes with him today.'

'Right, staying with Jayden Green. I'll send an email out and make sure everyone knows, don't you worry!'

Mr Cuthbert sounded extra keen to impress – he probably didn't get many direct instructions from the headteacher! He didn't even ask any questions about the exchange programme.

Alisha would have to remember this trick. If there hadn't been bigger issues at stake, she'd have asked Copy to cancel her after-school meeting as well.

They'd decided to say Copy was staying with Jayden, because his parents worked several jobs and were hard to get hold of on the phone. Jayden said the receptionists wouldn't attempt to ring his mum and dad unless they absolutely had to, as they knew how long it could take. Hopefully that meant no one from school would be ringing Jayden's parents to ask questions about Copy and his 'exchange programme'!

'All sorted,' said Mr Cuthbert. 'I'll just need Cop's last name?'

The copy-headteacher didn't reply. He stood very still, as if that would stop the receptionist from seeing him. Alisha and Jayden exchanged a worried look. They hadn't discussed this. Copy wouldn't know what to say. Maybe he didn't even know what a last name was!

'His last name is Eee,' Jayden piped up.

Mr Cuthbert looked sceptical. '*Eee?* And how's that spelt?'

'It's just, er, three Es,' said Jayden. The copy-headteacher nodded, as if he'd known that all along.

'Cop. Eee,' said Mr Cuthbert slowly, writing it down. 'How... different.'

'He's from Canada,' said Jayden, as if that explained everything.

'Goodbye,' said Copy, like they'd instructed him to once he'd said everything he needed to Mr Cuthbert. He walked abruptly away from the reception desk, followed by Jayden and Alisha. They left Mr Cuthbert behind looking bewildered, but the plan seemed to have worked!

Alisha and Jayden followed Copy out. A few students were hanging around by the basketball court but hurried off when they saw the copy-headteacher – thinking they'd be told off for being late for registration if they didn't!

'Did I do it right?' asked Copy. It was strange to hear Mr Hail's voice sounding so anxious.

'You were great,' Alisha reassured him. 'Which is more I can say for Jayden! *His last name is Eee!?*'

'Hey, I didn't hear you coming up with anything!' protested Jayden. 'And next time Grace comes up with a plan, she can be the one who – '

Jayden froze mid-sentence. Alisha followed his gaze, then gasped. The real Mr Hail was standing at a window, looking shocked at his mirror image standing outside. The real headteacher disappeared from sight, heading towards the double doors out on to the playground.

'Quick!' said Alisha, pushing Copy into a gap between two school buildings. 'You need to transform!'

WHOOOSH. In a rush of silver smoke, Copy turned back into his young-boy form. He looked like a mix of The Late Crew once more. They stepped out from between the buildings just in time to nearly walk into the headteacher.

'Alisha Alva. Jayden Green.' Mr Hail looked at Copy, and seemed embarrassed to see a student whose name he didn't know. 'And, um … you. Have you seen…'

'Seen what, sir?' asked Alisha innocently.

'Well, erm… I thought I saw…' stammered the headteacher, before composing himself. 'Never mind. I must have been confused. Anyway, the bell went five minutes ago. Get yourselves to registration.'

The three of them gratefully slipped away, leaving Mr Hail behind muttering to himself about how he needed a very long holiday.

A REAL BAD CASE OF THE HEEBIE-JEEBIES

Alisha sat in Maths, listening to pens scratching in notebooks. She couldn't concentrate on the exercise. She kept wondering if Copy was managing to fit in.

At breaktime, Jayden had said it was going OK – and that he'd told Copy to avoid answering any questions in class, just like he did. It was such a typical Jayden thing to say, but Alisha couldn't disagree that it was good advice!

However, it wasn't the teachers she worried would make things difficult for Copy.

She'd already overheard Patsy asking if anyone had spoken to 'Cop from Canada' yet. If Patsy met Copy, she'd want to ask him a million and one questions, so she could gossip about his answers. Fingers crossed, the alien would be lucky enough to avoid her all day!

Alisha felt heat creep up the back of her neck, as if someone was staring at her. She checked over her shoulder, but the rest of the class were working on the sums she was meant to be doing too.

Then she remembered what Copy had said about Difference Machines. *You can feel when one is watching you.* She peered out of the window, unsure what to search for. There were the school sheds, with green hills behind them. Then she spotted it, on top of one of the hills!

A red light, like an aeroplane's or a car's rear light, with a blurry grey shape behind it. Roughly as tall as a person and shaped like an upside-down triangle. It had to be the Difference Machine.

Everyone else kept their heads down, puzzling over Maths problems. No one else seemed to be feeling the itching sensation of being watched, like Alisha was. Which meant that the Difference Machine was only looking at her. She gulped. That wasn't good.

'Have you seen it?' demanded Alisha at lunchtime. She'd found Copy, Jayden, Tyler and Grace outside by the school field. The red light was still at the top of the nearby hill.

'Yeah,' said Jayden. 'Stupid light. It gives me the heebie-jeebies.'

Normally Alisha would have made fun of him for the phrase *heebie-jeebies*, but he was one hundred percent right!

'It was only watching us, wasn't it?' asked Tyler. 'Because no one else in my class seemed to be feeling the, uh, heebie-jeebies.'

The others nodded glumly.

'It's found enough difference to keep scanning us,' said Copy, his voice trembling. He must have been really afraid. 'It must know we're all behaving strangely.

But it doesn't know what I am yet. It would come closer if it did.'

'We're trying not to look at it too often,' Grace said to Alisha. 'We don't want the Machine to pick up that we're more interested in it than other people.'

Alisha nodded. It made sense. Other pupils might notice the red light on top of the hill, but it wouldn't be something that particularly grabbed their attention. She deliberately looked away from the Difference Machine, towards the school instead. Unfortunately, another problem was making its way towards them.

'Oh no,' gasped Alisha. 'Patsy Whitley's coming!'

'Ugh, anyone but her,' muttered Jayden.

For once, Alisha agreed with Jayden's complaining! Patsy marched over, flanked by her gossipy friends, Phoebe and Jake. They'd want to ask Copy *everything* about Canada. It was the last thing the alien needed – especially with the Difference Machine watching.

'Cop!' said Patsy, stopping with Phoebe and Jake on either side of her, like she was a celebrity and they were her security. 'You're from Canada, right? My uncle lives there. Where in Canada are you from?'

'Um…' said Copy, shrinking behind Alisha. She tried to think of something, *anything*, to say to get rid of Patsy and her friends. Then she felt that uncomfortable tingle on the back of her neck again, as if she was being spied on from afar. The Difference Machine's red eye was focused on her again, **right now**.

There was nothing Alisha could do. If she behaved in any way out of the ordinary, it'd only attract the Machine's attention even more. They were going to have to let Patsy and her friends ask Copy a bunch of questions about where he was from. But The Late Crew hadn't prepared Copy for that. He didn't know a single thing about Canada!

THE BRAND-NEW CANADA QUIZ SHOW

'Vancouver!' chipped in Grace, after the silence stretched too long.

Thank goodness for Grace and all the books she read! Alisha didn't know the names of any places in Canada – and looking at Tyler and Jayden's faces, she was certain that the boys didn't either.

Patsy flicked her hair. 'I wasn't asking *you*.'

'I'm from Vancouver,' stuttered Copy, sounding incredibly nervous.

Copy responding to that first question set them off. Pasty, Phoebe and Jake all started firing Canada-related questions at the alien. Alisha and the others could only watch on helplessly.

'Do you have the same lessons at school

in Canada? Do you have to listen to the national anthem at the start of the day?' asked Jake.

'What's Canadian food like? Do you eat maple syrup with everything?' asked Phoebe.

'Is it really cold in the snow? Do you ever go skiing or play ice hockey?' asked Patsy.

'Do Canadians really say sorry all the time?' asked Jake.

Copy looked completely lost, like he didn't understand half of the words they were saying. How was an alien supposed to know what a national anthem was? Or maple syrup, skiing and ice hockey? Alisha didn't even know if Copy had ever seen snow. Maybe they didn't have it on his planet.

'I-I...' Copy stammered.

Alisha felt another shiver run down her spine. Copy must have felt it too, because he glanced towards the hill and his eyes grew wide. Alisha followed his gaze and saw what they'd been dreading. The red light of the Difference Machine was moving down the hill towards them!

'That light's weird,' said Patsy, completely unaware of the terror it was causing them. 'But come on, Cop, tell us about Canada.'

Copy looked at Patsy, then at the Difference Machine coming down the hill, then at The Late Crew. He started to breathe very, very fast. It was almost like he couldn't bring in enough air. Without warning, the alien suddenly bolted away from them, running as fast as he could!

'All we did was ask about Canada!' exclaimed Patsy. 'You could have told us that he was so shy!'

Alisha, Tyler, Jayden and Grace ignored her, turning and chasing after their friend instead. As they ran off, they could hear Patsy, Phoebe and Jake talking in loud voices about how weird they all were. Ahead, Copy was already darting out of sight round the corner of the history classrooms.

'We need to – ' Alisha started to say. She stopped as she saw a pigeon fly up over the roof of the building that Copy had just disappeared behind. The bird flapped off in a hurried panic over their heads.

The red light descending the hill paused for a moment. Then the Difference Machine continued in a new direction, following the pigeon.

'We have to go after Copy,' Alisha said to the others. 'And I think I know where he's headed.'

CHASE THAT ALIEN!

'Where's he going then?' asked Tyler, as they all hurried down the steps out the front of Morfield Secondary school.

'He flew towards Morfield Woods,' said Alisha. 'He's going back to his spaceship.'

'But he can't just leave!' gasped Grace. 'What if we never see him again?'

'We don't know if he'll actually manage to lift off before the Difference Machine gets there,' added Alisha. 'Even if he does, it'll follow him wherever he goes – and he said it's faster than his ship. We've got to get to Morfield Woods first, and stop that robot once and for all!'

'How do we stop it?' asked Tyler.

'Ermmm,' stalled Alisha. 'I haven't worked that part out yet.'

'Well, great,' snorted Jayden. 'That's about as much of a plan as we ever have.'

'Are we just going to ditch school halfway through the day?' asked Grace anxiously. They'd already left the building behind, thankfully unnoticed by any teachers.

Alisha almost laughed. She couldn't believe *that* was what Grace was worrying about. Though actually, with her after-school meeting that day, she could really do without being in trouble for skipping the last two lessons.

'We've still got most of lunch left,' said Alisha unconvincingly. 'Maybe we'll be back in time.'

The rest of them looked at her with unimpressed expressions. She had to admit it seemed pretty unlikely they'd be back for the school bell.

'I'm going to go this way, to get Levi from Morfield Primary,' said Tyler, pointing down a different street. 'I'll make some excuse about why he's leaving early.

He'd never forgive me if I left him out! Plus, last time he was the one who worked out how to stop the evil slime.'

'We need Levi if we're going to stop the Difference Machine,' said Alisha, nodding. 'You go and pick him up, and the rest of us will get to Morfield Woods as fast as we can!'

SPINNING TOPS
USED TO BE FUN

Alisha, Jayden and Grace made their way down towards Morfield Woods. It was a clear day, the sky a cool blue above them. It was weather that would have been nice to be out in together, if they hadn't been so worried about Copy. Alisha hoped they'd be able to find him, and that the Difference Machine hadn't got there first.

'I still can't believe we snuck out of school,' said Grace again.

This time Alisha did laugh out loud. '*I* can't believe you're still thinking about that!'

'Don't get me wrong, I'm more concerned about Copy. But I've never misbehaved like this!'

'We're bad influences on you,' said

Jayden, sounding very proud.

To Alisha's relief, they saw their alien friend coming out from the trees, carrying his meteor-like spaceship. The Difference Machine, for now, was nowhere to be seen.

'Copy!' exclaimed Alisha. 'What are you doing?'

He looked up at them, tears running down his cheeks. Alisha found it weird to notice again that the alien's eyes were an exact replica of Grace's. His face just seemed like his own to her now – the face of her friend.

'I'm leaving,' Copy replied, his voice croaky after crying. 'I shouldn't have brought the Difference Machine here. You've all been so kind to me, and I've put you in danger.'

'But if you leave Earth, it'll just keep following you,' Alisha argued, trying to persuade him to stay. 'And the next place you go, there might not be anyone there to help you.'

Copy shrugged, though he couldn't hide

how frightened he looked. 'At least then I won't be bringing you all trouble. Now go, before the Difference Machine gets here.'

'Too late,' said Jayden, behind them.

Alisha spun around. The Difference Machine was following the edge of Morfield Woods, levitating a few centimetres above the ground. It looked like a giant spinning top, built from circles of metal rotating at different speeds. The red eye was on the highest disk, pointing directly towards Copy.

The Difference Machine's base was a sharp point that hovered in the air, the grass bending below it as if squashed down by some invisible force. Five mechanical arms protruded from a non-spinning part at the robot's centre. They ended in:

- a radar dish
- an antennae
- something that looked like a laser pen
- robot claw (small)
- robot claw (large).

The robot advanced towards Copy, its mechanical arms rising up threateningly like scorpion tails. The light from its red eye glowed on the alien boy's shirt.

'Now would be a really good time to come up with that plan,' Jayden whispered to Alisha out of the side of his mouth.

AN OUT-OF-THIS-WORLD PLAN!

A white beam shot out from the *something that looked like a laser pen*, blasting into Copy. A fuzzy ball of energy formed around their alien friend. Copy was dragged up into the air, and then began to be reeled in towards the robot. It was like the Difference Machine was a fisherman ... and Copy was the fish!

'It's got a tractor beam!' shouted Grace.

Alisha and Jayden both looked at her, surprised.

'What?' asked Grace. 'I watch sci-fi shows too. I know what a tractor beam is.'

Copy struggled as he was pulled closer to the Difference Machine, but couldn't free himself. He closed his eyes tight and clenched his hands, like he was trying to transform. Somehow, the tractor beam was stopping him!

'We've got to help him!' Jayden shouted desperately, abandoning his usual act of being too tough to care about anything.

Alisha stooped down, grabbed a rock from the ground, and threw it as hard as she could at the Difference Machine, aiming for the red eye.

Ping! It bounced off one of the spinning metal circles, with absolutely no effect.

Ping! Ping! Jayden and Grace threw their own rocks. Grace even hit the red light, but their stones just bounced off the Machine as well. They weren't going to stop this alien technology with brute force!

'It scans based on difference!' yelled Tyler. He and Levi had arrived, rushing down the hill towards them. 'Levi says we need something even more different to distract it!'

The brothers stopped next to the rest of The Late Crew, panting. They all looked on in horror, as the robot slowly tractor-beamed Copy through the air towards itself.

'How do we make something even more different?' asked Alisha urgently.

'I don't know,' replied Levi, looking like he was trying really hard to think of something. 'That's as far as I've got.'

The metal disks that made up the Difference Machine opened, revealing a cage inside. It was going to pull Copy in, unless they did something to stop it!

An idea popped into Alisha's head. It was the sort of thing that Mum would do. She was pretty sure it was ridiculous, but she had to try. She leapt forward and did an impression of an alien, taking huge steps and making *zeep-zoop* noises.

For a moment, nothing happened. She kept on *zeeping* and *zooping* around the grass, hoping desperately that it would work. The rest of The Late Crew stared at her, utterly dumbfounded as to what on Earth – or what on any other planet! – she was doing. Alisha felt like an idiot, but didn't stop. Copy needed her.

The red eye spun round towards Alisha, and she felt that shudder that meant the Difference Machine was looking at her. She *zeep-zooped* as loud as she could, and Copy stopped in the air. He wasn't free from the tractor beam, but he wasn't being pulled any closer either.

Levi was the first to cotton on to what Alisha was doing.

'I AM AN ALIEN!' he announced in a funny voice, and shuffled around like a penguin. The red eye turned towards Levi. The tractor beam weakened for a second, almost dropping Copy to the ground. The Machine was confused!

Tyler, Jayden and Grace all started doing their own alien impressions. Tyler ran fast and spun his arms, Jayden pretended to be a monkey creature on all fours, and Grace spoke an alien-style language that she was making up on the spot.

The Machine scanned for difference – so they'd give it all the difference it could handle! The red light turned faster and faster, unable to decide which one to focus on. There was a *crrr-UNCH* sound inside the robot. Its tractor beam suddenly released Copy, and the alien landed on his bum on the grass.

'Error,' said the Difference Machine's deep computerised voice. There was a hiss to its speakers, like it was coming out of an old TV monitor or radio. The Difference Machine could talk, and it was speaking English!

ACTUALLY, IT WAS BETTER WHEN THE SCARY ROBOT DIDN'T TALK

'Identify the shapeshifter,' ordered the Difference Machine.

The Late Crew all stopped, halfway through alien impressions. Alisha had a fleeting thought that if anyone took a photo of them at that moment, they'd all look pretty strange. Then it dawned on her, the machine had told them to *identify the shapeshifter* – that meant it was no longer sure which of them was the alien!

'No way!' shouted Tyler.

'Yeah, what are you going to do about it?' joined in Jayden. He sounded cocky now their alien impersonations had stopped the Difference Machine in its tracks.

'More Difference Machines will be summoned to your planet. The shapeshifter will be found.'

Alisha groaned. Why did Jayden think it was a good idea to taunt the space robot? Then her heart sunk even lower as Copy began to climb to his feet. The alien was going to give himself up! She couldn't let that happen.

'Our friend deserves to be free,' Alisha said, staring into the Difference Machine's red eye and refusing to look away. 'If you and your planet can't see that, it's your problem. Not his.'

To her side, she saw Copy moving again. He lifted his hand, and she thought he still might surrender. Then he put his fingers on his head, like they were his bizarre hair, and did a walk that reminded Alisha of a chicken. He was an alien, doing an impression of an alien!

Of course – the Difference Machine

had deliberately distracted them from doing their alien impressions. The robot had wanted them to stop because the impressions were making it malfunction.

The Late Crew all followed Copy's lead and pretended to be aliens again, circling their funny walks around the robot. Alisha *zeep-zooped* and heard everyone else making their own strange noises.

Zeep-zoop!
  Brrrrrooooooak!
    Mwwwwaaaaarrrg!
      Ssszzzzssssszzzzsszzzurp!
     Clorp-a-dorp!
       Aweeeeepooooooooo!

It was all too much for the Difference Machine. A whistling sound came out from somewhere, and smoke began rising out of the gaps between its disks. There was a smell like burning eggs, and then a **CRACK** and a *SNA-A-P!*

The Difference Machine wobbled, its

disks spinning faster and faster, and looser and looser – before one in the middle *pinged* out, smacking into a tree! The robot fell apart as it crashed down into the ground. A couple of the disks rolled away like coins, clattering on to their sides on the grass.

'We did it!' said Alisha, punching the air in celebration.

'Great plan, in the end,' Jayden said to her. 'I'd have never thought to pretend to be an alien.'

'Well, it was Levi's idea really. He said we needed something more different than Copy, to distract the Difference Machine. I just guessed that acting more alien than the real alien might fit the bill!'

'Thank you all,' said Copy. 'You saved me.'

Alisha let out a relieved sigh. They had beaten the Difference Machine, and everything felt pretty perfect. Of course, that was when the next thing happened.

'Xzorysssnoripipoxitizxyxl?

Xzorysssnoripipoxitizxyxl?' said a
voice that Alisha had never heard
before. But she did recognise that long,
strange word. Where did she know it
from? Then she realised what it was.
Xzorysssnoripipoxitizxyxl was Copy's real
name, in his alien language. Someone was
calling out Copy's real name!

THE LONG
DISTANCE CALL

'I know that voice,' said Copy.

He walked over to his meteor-like spaceship. Alisha realised that was where the mysterious voice was coming from! The Late Crew gathered round as Copy ducked down and placed his hand on the ship. The stone surface glowed yellow. A small hologram of an alien appeared on top of it, about the size of a mouse standing upright on its hind legs.

The new alien looked like it really was perched on top of Copy's ship – except they could see through its body to the trees of Morfield Wood! The creature had blue skin and grey clothes. It was human-shaped, other than insectoid eyes and webbed six-fingered hands. It flapped its hands together in a way that made Alisha think it was worried.

'Xzorysssnoripipoxitizxyxl? Xzorysssnoripipoxitizxyxl?' the holographic alien repeated.

'Who's that?' asked Alisha.

'My mother-parent,' Copy answered sadly. He looked like he wanted to hug the hologram, but Alisha guessed his arms would pass straight through. She couldn't imagine how lonely he must feel, having been away from his own planet for so long.

'Can she see us?' asked Grace.

'No,' replied Copy. 'She can't see or hear us unless I answer the call. She won't even know I'm standing here.'

'Is that what you look like normally? Like, uh, that size?' said Jayden, focusing on completely the wrong thing. Though Alisha couldn't deny she was interested too!

'Yes, that's our actual size. It's been strange, being bigger.'

'Are you going to answer her call?' asked Tyler.

Copy didn't reply. His eyebrows (copies of Alisha's!) scrunched downwards, like he was confused and didn't know what to do.

'The signal for this call travelled all the way between the two planets,' said Levi, staring at the hologram in fascination. 'It's amazing that your species can do that. But if you answer, your mum will know you're a shapeshifter.'

Of course – Copy was still in his human form!

'Didn't you think your parents might already have guessed?' asked Tyler.

'Yes,' replied Copy. 'Like I said, they might even have been the ones who sent the Difference Machine after me. But I don't know for sure.'

'Can you still not turn back?' Alisha asked.

Copy tensed, trying to transform. A weak cloud of silver smoke puffed out of him, but he stayed human.

'I still can't,' moaned Copy. 'I can become anything, apart from myself.'

Alisha thought about how hard she found it to tell people about being a young carer, and how she'd disliked the idea of being marked out as 'different'. And that was just in school – Copy was worried about his own mum seeing him differently, and maybe even hating his shapeshifting powers.

'You've got nothing to be ashamed of,' said Alisha. 'Your ability to transform is amazing. We can't control how your mum reacts to it. But whatever happens, we'll still be your friends.'

'Thanks, Alisha,' said Copy. He sounded like it meant a lot to him. Then he took a deep breath and answered the call, still looking like a human.

'Xzorysssnoripipoxitizxyxl?' Copy's mum asked, and Alisha knew she could see him now.

'Zzryp,' Copy replied, which Alisha guessed meant yes.

Copy's mum started speaking very fast in the alien language, so quickly that

Alisha couldn't tell where there were words, and where there were pauses. Occasionally, Copy would reply, speaking in the same alien language.

Alisha watched her friend's face, but she couldn't quite tell what he was feeling. It looked like everything all at once: fear, relief, sadness, excitement. She wondered what his mum was saying to him.

Slow curls of silver smoke started to rise up from Copy's skin. Tyler moved forward, but Levi pulled him back.

'No, I think it's OK,' Levi said to his brother.

Then something magical began.

THE TRANSFORMATION

Unlike Copy's other transformations, this one happened in stages. Thin wisps of the silver smoke swirled around his body, transparent enough so that they could still see him as he changed.

1. His skin took on a light grey tinge, before darkening to the colour of blueberries.
2. He shrank, his clothes changing from a Morfield Secondary school uniform to grey fabrics like his mother wore.
3. His eyes spread out into two compound domes, like those of an ant or fly.

4. His five fingers became six, with
   frog-like webbing appearing between
   them.

When he finished, he was even smaller than
his mother. He climbed up his spaceship,
his webbed fingers and toes sticking to the
surface. He stopped once he reached the
hologram of his mum at the top.

'Copy, you're... *you*!' exclaimed Alisha.

Copy, now a small blue alien, said
something to his mother in their language,
then pressed his hand to the asteroid
spaceship. The hologram of his mother
froze, but did not disappear. Copy turned
back to The Late Crew.

'I've paused the call,' said Copy. He
sounded squeaky now he was little – this
was their first time hearing his real voice!
'Yes, I'm me. Telling the truth about who
I am made me feel free, and I was able to
transform back.'

'What did your mum say?' Grace asked,
tentatively. Alisha knew she was worried

that Copy's mother might have said something awful to him, now that she'd seen him transformed into a human.

'She and Father-Parent worked out that I ran away because I'm a shapeshifter,' said Copy. There was glittering golden liquid at the bottom of his compound eyes, which Alisha thought might be tears. 'But they didn't send the Difference Machine.'

'If they didn't, who did?' asked Jayden.

'A teacher from my school-pod,' Copy said sadly. 'Which is still horrible. But at least it wasn't my parents.'

'So, what now?' asked Alisha.

'Mother-Parent said that people on Xoxorathia-Zarapa-Vee were shocked by my story, that a child my age chose to run away from our planet. There's some pod-towns that are refusing to let Difference Machines in. She wants me to come back and tell everyone why they should be kinder to shapeshifters.'

'Will you go back?' asked Tyler.

'Yes,' said Copy. He sounded determined.

'I want to speak out. I want to change how everyone sees shapeshifters and make life better for the next child like me.'

'Wow,' gasped Grace. 'You're going to fight to make a difference. You've gone from a shapeshifter to a mind-shifter!'

Copy's small blue shoulders dropped, his confidence falling away a little.

'I'll need to start close to home,' he said. 'She said Father-Parent loves me and wants me to come back. But he's finding it difficult that I'm a shapeshifter. He might be the first person I have to persuade that this power can be a good thing.'

'Your power is wonderful, Copy,' said Alisha. 'And you're a wonderful person.'

She normally hated being soppy, but sometimes you just had to be!

'Thank you, The Late Crew,' said Copy, his high-pitched voice squeaking with emotion. 'If I do manage to change minds on my home planet, it's because you all helped me to change my mind about myself. Now, I'm going to talk to Mother-

Parent more. I think you need to go back to your school-pod?'

'Oh no!' cried Grace. 'It's five minutes till lunch is over! We're going to be late!'

After making Copy promise to meet them later, and not leave without saying goodbye, The Late Crew rushed back towards Morfield Secondary School – which was definitely more than five minutes away, no matter how fast they ran!

IN CASE OF EMERGENCY, PRETEND TO BE DISTRACTED BY A FROG

Alisha rushed into her science lesson, miraculously only five minutes late. At least it would seem like she'd been on the school grounds! Jayden and Grace would probably get away with it too, though she felt sorry for Tyler. He'd had to take Levi back to Morfield Primary first. There was no way he wasn't going to be in trouble.

'Ahem.' Mr McNulty raised his eyebrows as Alisha shuffled past classmates to get to her seat. She ignored Patsy staring at her from the other side of the room.

'Sorry I'm late, sir.' There was only one thing for it – distraction! And she knew the perfect topic. 'But camouflage is the reason I'm late.'

Mr McNulty put on a sceptical expression but couldn't hide the interest in his voice. 'Oh really? And how exactly did camouflage delay you in getting to your lesson?'

'Well sir, I've always wanted a pet frog,' said Alisha, making it up as she went along. 'Today, I saw the perfect green frog by the school field. I snuck up, ready to catch it in my lunchbox, when – *poof!* It hopped into the grass and completely vanished. I looked for it all lunchtime, but it was like it had turned invisible. And since then, I haven't been able to stop thinking about how amazing an invisible frog would be!'

'I have no doubt that this didn't actually happen, and I know you're far too intelligent to attempt to take a wild frog home in your lunchbox...' Mr McNulty began, and Alisha cringed, certain she was going to get told off.

But then the teacher added, 'However, I will give you points for inventiveness. And you raise an interesting point, that many British animals use camouflage too. For example, the hedgehog, which appears similar to mud or earth. A good activity is to keep your eye out for local wildlife and examine how they are camouflaged...'

And with that, Mr McNulty was off, Alisha's lateness completely forgotten!

Alisha sat outside Miss Penn's office at the end of the day, thinking about Copy while she waited for Mum to arrive. She hoped he'd be happy on Xoxorathia-Zarapa-Vee, and that things there would change for the better.

'You know, I considered bringing Hugo,' said Mum, walking down the corridor towards Alisha. 'As emotional support for us both. But I don't think he's very good at meetings.'

Alisha grinned. 'I don't think *I'm* very good at meetings.'

'Neither am I.' Mum winked. 'But we'll get through it together. Maybe it would help if I pretended to be German?'

'What!?' asked Alisha. That was the last thing she'd expected to come out of Mum's mouth.

'I remember a bit of German from school. I could say *Alisha ist sehr gut*. That means Alisha is very good.'

'Muuu*uuuum*.'

At that moment, Miss Penn opened the door. She looked a little confused as to why Alisha and Mum were both trying to control fits of giggles.

'Er, hello,' said the Head of Year. 'Are you ready to come in?'

'*Ja*,' Mum said. Alisha tried to shoot her a withering glare but couldn't keep the smirk from her own face!

NO BIG DEALS, PLEASE

In the office, Miss Penn sat across from Alisha and Mum.

'We're here to talk about you being tired in school,' said Miss Penn. 'You're not in trouble, Alisha. We just want to work out ways we can help. It's probably best to start with asking why you think you've been so exhausted?'

Miss Penn had asked her this question before, and she hadn't properly answered. A voice in her mind told her to do the same again and pretend to be a ♫ *normal perfectly proper girl* ♫ so the Head of Year would leave her alone. She didn't think Mum would reveal the truth if she did.

But she remembered Copy, bravely explaining who he was to his alien mother.

Then she thought about Mum saying she should be proud of who she was.

'I'm a young carer for Mum,' said Alisha, surprising herself with her own bluntness. 'You know Mum has her Letters – her EUPD. Some nights, I need to stay up with her to make sure she's OK. I haven't talked about this at school, because I'm worried I'll be treated differently. Or that people will think Mum's a bad parent, because of her mental health.'

'I'm actually a great parent,' Mum interjected cheerfully, which made Alisha smile. Even Miss Penn's mouth lifted up at one side.

'Mum and I are working on me not staying up so late,' continued Alisha. 'The best way for school to help is by not making a big deal out of it. If teachers understand why I might sometimes be tired, and don't treat me or Mum differently than anyone else, then I'll be happy.'

Alisha let out a deep breath. That was the longest she'd ever spoken about herself in an actually serious way. Mum looked proud of her. Miss Penn seemed impressed as well, as far as Alisha could tell.

'Thank you for telling me that,' said Miss Penn, speaking unusually gently. 'That all makes a lot of sense. It's not nice to have to worry about you or your family being treated unfairly. I think we can support you in the way you want, without making a big deal out of it. I do have one question though.'

'What's that?' Alisha asked.

Miss Penn arched one eyebrow. 'When you say you want to be treated the same as everyone else, does that include being told off when you're making too many jokes in class?'

Alisha and Mum both burst out laughing. Who knew that Miss Penn had a sense of humour!

JAYDEN ACTUALLY SAYS SOMETHING POSITIVE

Getting into the car after the meeting, Alisha felt pretty happy. To be fair to Miss Penn, she'd actually made some helpful suggestions. Like if Alisha struggled to keep up with homework when Mum was having Bad Nights, she could let her teacher know and she'd get extra time to complete it. That was better than getting in trouble for not finishing the work!

'That Miss Penn's alright,' said Mum. 'Though she's a bit stiff. I did wonder if she might be a robot.'

Alisha didn't respond to that. After the Difference Machine, she'd had quite enough robots for one lifetime!

'Well, I think you deserve it,' announced Mum, as she drove away from the school. 'Your ChocoHut ban is officially lifted! Do you want to head there now?'

'Actually, it's Cop's last night here,' said Alisha sadly. She couldn't believe the alien would soon be gone. 'Would you mind dropping me off at Grace's house? So I can say goodbye.'

'Of course. Is Cop going back to Canada then?'

'Yes,' replied Alisha. 'And Canada feels like it's light years away...'

Alisha and Grace met Tyler, Levi and Jayden by the edge of Morfield Woods. It was getting dark, and the first few stars were twinkling in the sky. The boys explained they'd already seen Copy, and that the alien had gone into the woods to get his spaceship.

Apparently, they'd got Copy to call the school reception, doing his exact imitation of Mr Hail's voice. He'd told Mr Cuthbert that Cop was returning to Canada immediately because of an emergency.

'Did you get in trouble for being back late?' Grace asked Tyler.

'Detention tomorrow,' sighed Tyler.

'Detention isn't too bad,' said Jayden. 'We all met in detention!'

'That's the most positive thing you've ever said,' Alisha replied, smirking at Jayden. 'And it was about the time the school almost fell on us.'

Copy emerged in his human form, carrying his meteorite ship out from the woods. He put it down between them all.

'I thought you might like to see me as a human one last time,' he said. 'Also, I can't pick up the ship when I'm in my own body, I'm too small!'

'You're welcome to come back and be human whenever you want,' said Grace.

'You'll always be an honorary member of The Late Crew,' said Tyler.

'And our favourite shapeshifter,' added Levi.

'As well as a butt-kicking Difference Machine smasher!' said Jayden, doing a karate chop and a kick.

'You're our friend, Copy,' said Alisha softly. 'And that's enough, all on its own.'

Though Copy was smiling, she saw tears in his eyes. Then gradually, those tears changed colour to gold. The silver smoke rolled out of his body, and he shifted down into his small alien shape. He climbed into his asteroid, stopping before he was fully inside.

'I'll return one day,' the alien vowed. 'Once I've made Xoxorathia-Zarapa-Vee a better place for shapeshifters. I'll come back and tell you all about it.'

He ducked out of view, disappearing into the asteroid. The Late Crew all stared at the ship expectantly. They waited. Nothing happened.

'Is it going to, uh … *do something*?' asked Tyler.

WHHHHHIIIIIRRRRRRRRR!

The beachball-sized rock began to

vibrate in the ground. It kicked dirt up around it, shaking on the spot faster and faster. It began to glow, molten orange, with steam rising from the holes. Alisha could feel the heat on her face, like standing in front of a bonfire.

Then *BOOM!* it shot into the air in a blast of orange light, streaking away through the sky like a shooting star. It left a patch of smouldering burnt grass behind.

'Does that count as "*doing something*"?' Jayden asked Tyler.

HUGO STILL
AVOIDS MIRRORS

That night, Alisha sat in her bedroom, an
empty ChocoHut cup on her desk. Mum
knew Alisha was sad as soon she picked
her up from Grace's house, where The
Late Crew went after Copy left. Mum had
insisted on visiting the ChocoHut drive-
through on the way home, to cheer
Alisha up.

The warm chocolatey drink did make her
feel a bit better. The amusing thought of
Mr Hail's confusion when he found out *he*
had called the school yesterday to say 'Cop'
was going home to Canada, helped too.

Of course, there was a certain cat
who could always make her smile. Hugo
peeked out from under her desk, glancing
cautiously around. Alisha knew he was

225

looking out for his mirror image.

'There's no copy creatures,' Alisha reassured the cat. 'And it turned out the one we met was very nice.'

Hugo looked at her doubtfully, but still leapt up when she patted her knee. He purred when she stroked him, and settled down on her lap. Alisha gazed out of the window, up towards the stars. She wondered if one of them was actually the light of Copy's spaceship, getting further and further from Earth.

'It's a funny old universe, Hugo,' she whispered. 'There are people who won't like you just for being who you are. Because you're a shapeshifter, or you have Letters, or for any other reason they can think of.'

She looked down at the black-and-white cat on her legs.

'But then there's people who'll love you for who you are as well. And cats, who don't care about any of it. And the universe can't be too bad...'

Hugo raised his head towards her, his green eyes glinting. He might not understand the words she said, but he really did listen.

'… if it's got cats in it.'

Create your own alien

Use the questions below to make up your own alien, and create your own alien adventure!

What is your alien's name, and the name of its species?

What is its special power, and how does it use it?

What does it look, sound, and smell like?

Why does it visit Earth, and who does it meet there?